T0129234

IN BETWEEN
TWO CENTURIES

Published novels:

"A journey without address" 2013
"Trails of the night"2014

Volumes of poetry:

"Life has one direction" 2011
"Monologue of a refugee" 2016

Other books:

"Memoirs, articles, reportage reviews and literary analysis" 2012
"Street without address" 2013
"Tear of the Chamëria" 2016
"Proud of Arbery" 2016
"With Albanians of Presevo League in Canada" 2018
"Word has got me stuck" 2019
"With the Albanians of Canada" 2019

IN BETWEEN TWO CENTURIES

THREE NOVELE

Mustafe Ismaili

IN BETWEEN TWO CENTURIES
THREE NOVELE

iUniverse books may be ordered through booksellers or by contacting:

iUniverse
1663 Liberty Drive
Bloomington, IN 47403
www.iuniverse.com
1-800-Authors (1-800-288-4677)

ISBN: 978-1-5320-8033-3 (sc)
ISBN: 978-1-5320-8034-0 (e)

Library of Congress Control Number: 2019911924

Print information available on the last page.

iUniverse rev. date: 08/16/2019

The greatest slavery is living away of your homeland. There is where my soul and blood belong. The sun doesn't shine the same elsewhere.

MUSTAFE ISMAILI
Toronto Canada

Contents

Dedication

We can never delete our past. Principles and values remain and are transmitted for the rest of life the same bitter memories. But we can write our future. This is the truth I consider along my entire life.

This book is a dedication to my family, especially my nieces, "Eliza" for her fifth birthday, and "Elora" for her third birthday and for my grandson Elvis for his sixth month birthday.

You are always in my heart and I love you to the moon and back!

Your granddad!

Mustafë Ismaili

Preamble

A prose that explores the soul of an entire nation
About the latest novels of the author Mustafë Ismaili
Born in Preseva Valley, Resident in Toronto, Canada.

Written by Namik Selmani

I have considered the prose and poetry of Mustafë Ismaili very attentively, not solely in terms of friendship, but, more importantly, to be introduced to the entire literal works that have been created in Preseva Valley. Certainly, I have considered the love it transmits, how it has been written full of love; how the same love has been spread through words in the World of Literacy in Diaspore, part of which he is since 20 years ago. The auspicious thought that Diaspore provides the reader with as a social, political, cultural phenomenon is at the same time a mystery of the present and future Diaspore. Naturally, there are no written rules here, but it is widely known that unwritten rules have resisted significantly due to the force they give people in everyday life, not only seen from the individual viewpoint but from the collective one too. To be mentioned are groups or organizations of writers, sometimes well organized and financially secure because of their leaders who are mostly volunteers and at times less strong in such aspects. When I say that there are no written rules, certainly this refers to themes of these books. In his poetry, Mustafë Ismaili, this decent man of Preseva Valley, or the way I know and refer to it since many years ago: "The Valley of Albanian Letters" is creating a new literal tradition. Though it has been a long period of time, Mustafa has correctly and in a challenging way defined the tematics of his creations, in prose and poetry. Thus, surely we can say that in prose he is serious, productive and extremely narrative.

I attentively read the three novels with which he will be present to the numerous readers, in his hometown, in Albania, Kosovo and further, in Diaspore, Canada, where he currently lives. They are entitled: "In betwee two centuries" "Plan for eviction" and "Sami". The three of them are narrated in a typical Albanian setting and in the shape of a very beautiful bridge not only do they naturally connect places but also they give you the feeling of being a participant of the events, living the dramas and feeling the emotions of the characters. The novels have been placed in the Albanian landscape, but have been written in Toronto. This is the glorious award that he gives to himself for sharing writings in the Albanian language though two decades have passed. If we view at it in the metaphoric aspect, I would compare to a waterfall, the second great one after the Niagara. Thus, in front of the Niagara Waterfall, the waterfall of lettering in Albanian of the novels of M. Ismaili in the triple novels of this book is purest and much more shining than that natural beauty. The topic he treats in a professional detailed manner is the relationship of truths, trust between people in Albania and the Balcans. It treats the moral values that Albanians do have that apparently give him the Identity Passport in the great world outside. To such extent he is a very courageous creative writer. At the times when Europe was concerned about an almost imaginary conflict between different civilisations, he decides to provide the reader with some very interesting subjects. Here is where theestimation of the new book starts.

The novel "Plan for eviction" develops some events happening in a religious environment; precisely it joins two types of environments, the religious and educational. Established in a setting where religion has great influence, education raises against falsity which is normal and usual in between people who preach it. Two characters are essential in the novel Fati (In Albanian language means 'destiny') and Sadija. The choice of this name makes the author successful. It implies the symbolic of an entire life very often referred to, with this name. Good luck in studies, in getting a good marriage, in having children, in finding a job and so on. The next part of the conflict developped in the novel is that of generations. Not leaving behind the beautiful tradition of the region, approaching to the social, cultural, political and religious frame of the time, the author provides the reader with significant meassages in an impressively original way. The entire book has got special composition. There are three novels creating a single book in the shape of a roman. This is a particularity that hasn't been noticed in the recent years. The title also is symbolic. At first view, a distracted reader would notice a series of conflicts of a certain time, but seen deeply in bridges that connect centuries, there are conflicts between individuals, regions, states and beyond. The well-known author has managed to be the story teller of such problematic regions such as Preseva, Preseva Valley etc. The three novels introduce artistically: the pain, revolt against illiteracy, poverty, hate for the Slavic invador especially in this area where anti-Albanian activities have been widespread.

On the other hand the experience in the prose and roman is preminent for other author's successes in the field. This literal work puts him in the first line of best authors of Diaspore.

The creative motto he uses is enough for us to understand and believe that other works will be amazingly written by this author, honouring him and the entire Albanian literature. Truth is the way that should be followed all the life....

A great appraisal for the author is his serious attempt to introduce his works in English as well. This is evidence of a problem that has impeded Albanian authors to be recognized in the world's literature. This includes authors who are now trying to introduce their works in the respective countries where they live and work now: Germany, Italy, Greece, the USA, Canada, UK etc.It is not yet a tradition in our country, which personally I think depends on the financial situation, that literal works of this group of people are translated and published. This would not just be a linking bridge of nations and states they have migrated but an obligation for the young generations as well who have not yet had the opportunity of the massive Albanian literature in their houses.

Tirana, July 2019

Painful Biography

In the early spring, snow was converted into small streams of water coming fresh and beautiful from up the mountain, reaching the bottom, almost 500 meters in the village creating a river of amazingly crystal clear water which would then wind through fields and houses and end in the river Moravica. The river went through the Valley for a few kilometers until it reached the southern Morava. The amount of water in this river was appropriate for the watering of fields and gardens along its flow. Sometimes, during winter the river would get so terrifying due to the weather conditions and would surpass its banks, flooding without mercy the fields, meadows, gardens and everything else possible.

Starting from the late March, the villagers were committed to the activities in the fields where they did everything in a very well-organized way. They consulted one another, especially with the elderly as they obviously had much more experience in agriculture. They fertilized the fields in autumn and then they worked on them spreading all the dung in the entire surface of the fields.

They made good use of time as much as they could, because during this period of the year precipitations were frequent, and they could encounter difficulties because of humidity. As the melted snow entered deep in the ground and as soon as the soil dried, the villagers were asked to start their engagement in village works. Someone was needed to be attentive in order to observe and test the fields if they were appropriate to be worked on, so people of the village had chosen uncle Vela and Njiazi. They were considered as the best in the village, the ones who tested if the fields were appropriate for working on them. After the peak of working activities, the villagers would then do some works without any will or desire, just for the sake of work. Particularly they would deal with the construction works for the main road in the village. It was now a tradition that every spring before the special celebration of Saint Gjergj different activities for the good maintenance of the main road which separated the village in two parts, were held. These activities would last one day or two. This was definitely the witness for the villagers being real hard workers, well organized and dedicated to their blessed land. Always together they would help one another even in other jobs which were difficult to handle, especially to those families which needed men. If someone wanted to build a house or a barn or a stable for the stock everyone would be of good help in order to construct the facility the sooner and the better possible.

In this village there was a man called Bani. He had lost all his family thus he was lonely and suffered from mental disorder. The whole village took care of him as everyobody knew his problems. Each family in the village was responsible of the well-being of Bani, supplying him with food each week in turns, whereas, once in two weeks his sister who was married and living in another village would come and visit him. She would do a clear-out to the house he lived in, which had been constructed by the villagers, and she would do the laundry for the following two weeks. Bani was grateful for all the services were provided to him by the villagers and by his sister. This made the village well known in the area as a very humanitarian and well organized. It was considered an example to all the other villages around. Inhabitants here didn't belong to one tribe only, as it was usual in other villages. Their ancestors had been newcomers from different Albanian regions who had been evicted from the serbian-slavics. The chairmen of the village had accepted and recognized them as brothers and this was the reason why marriages within the village weren't allowed to occur. They preserved this brotherhood stating that if they did such marriages this strong relation would break down. This was very strongly perceived by the chairman as well, the oldest man in the village. He believed that if youngsters started getting married inside the village's families then this brotherhood would no longer exist, so he wanted people of his village to preserve this attitude as a precious tradition. There was no difficulty in matching the boys of the village as the best girls from very good families of the other villages came here. Consequently, healthy and strong relationships were established between these people. Education and well being were in the highest levels. Since never had there ever been any conflict among families in the village. In the center of the latter there was the mosque, built in oriental architecture and the beautiful proud minaree. It was a place where people never missed, especially youngsters and men, more frequently on Fridays, the most preferable day to pray to God! The chairman of the village often advised the youth to pray for the well continuance of their wonderful relationships within the village members. He feared that one day this peaceful atmosphere could be broken down. He often said: "I fear that one day I will not be here any longer and all this comfort I am leaving behind will get lost".

He also admitted to have proven some signs that things were about to change. He feared that maybe the tradition they had preserved until now would lose if the youth got education out of the religious traditions. The national issue was secondary in importance to the chairman. He couldn't go beyond the very strict religious ideology.

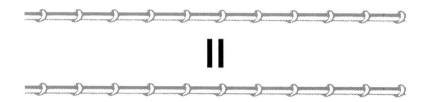

II

Very few villagers were educated, and very rare were those who could read and write, having finished the elementary school in the other village, Pallahang, 8km away. Only a few elderly men were able to write in the Arabic, Turkish and CyrillicAlphabetic letters.

Fati was one of those who studied in High School. The idea to get educated had been introduced by one of his uncles being conditioned by his sister. She absolutely wanted to see her son getting education. She wanted him to become a wise man in his future as she, herself, had suffered a lot, and had been a victim of this old tradition due to a system of ignorance andilliteracy.

Though she had dared to raise her voice and had constantly protested in front of her brothers for the matching-marriage against her will, she had found neither comprehension nor solution by them yet. Reluctantly she had become a victim of the patriarchal prejudice tradition. Since the beginning she had realised her marriage wouldn't be a good and happy one, eventually she had complained to her brothers assuring them and factuating them her words. To her misfortune, her brothers had reacted carelessly to her complaints. Moreover, they had asked her not to speak a word any longer, offending her and mistreating her. They had also obliged her to be quiet and to stay with her husband no matter what happened between them. They considered it would be a shame for the popular surname Bajraktari if she kept complaining about her marriage.

-May this be your last complaint- the oldest brother had yelled, sealing his words as if they were a military order.

In these conditions she had been obliged to accept the violence of her husband and the pressure from her brothers. As time passed by, her son grew old. As her son grew old, the hope of seeing him graduated one day grew. She begged her brothers in her knees:

-Please make possible the education of my son, otherwise I will never forgive all the pressure you have put on me all these years. The very times she met them she would complain on dissatisfaction and sufferings she had gone through since she had got married, but they had never reacted and never changed their decisions and they pressured her to keep the family united and accept the destiny she was gifted by God!

Very late did the brothers understand and accept the bitter reality. Now regret was inevitable. They apologised very pityful for everything but now it was too late.

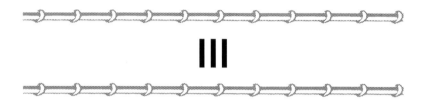

III

The environment where Fati grew up and got educated played a decisive role in his life development and inner feelings. His grandfather was a rich landowner who owned livestock and properties such as lands.

He was conservative and against education and emancipation, especially of the woman, though education was one of the main rights and duties of each citizen. He was totally against it. He imposed this to his son as well. It is said that he paid money so that his son wasn't accepted at school, because he had this conviction that school wasn't an appropriate place for Muslims. Fati's mother was an intelligent woman from a very well known Bajraktar family. This was the reason she had been given for marriage matching to this rich family. Fati was a child sorrounded by love and care from his mother. She was always very careful to him, observing every movement he did, whereas his father was a selfish man and very opinionated. His care was quite limited. He was a shepherd, very dedicated to the animals and he didn't spend time on other things except from the livestock. He spent most of his time in fields and mountains with the sheep. He had tried to learn how to play the flute but had resulted unsuccessful. He was tall, with an athletic body, very strong compared to the people of his age. He was the first in the village whenever there were any events or party organizations, weddings and other celebrations, or sometimes even sports activities: such as stone throwing and weightlifting and very courageous in fighting with the other shepherds of the village and other villages around. In sprinting he would always be the first to grab the winning prize. He was powerful physically. He drank either cow or goat milk without even boiling it. The same he did with eggs, he would break their shell and drink the entire egg. Apart from these qualities he was very agressive too. He was disobedient and did never accept advice from the elderly. He wasn't joyful; he didn't understand or accept jokes. He realized his threatenings. Everyone was scaredof him. However, in case anyone was in trouble because of any threaten by someone else they would go to him and ask him for help and he would always help so everyone tried to stay away from him. Never had anybody wished him "Good job!" Never had he done any other job except for the shepherd. He never socialized with people. He was unable to maintain and take care of his family. He didn't enjoy social life and community, but just being alone.

He was quite a unique person and it was extremely difficult to convince that great man, that's how he was described by most villagers. He had no comprehension with the co-villagers. He was difficult to understand and to handle. The consequences of these bad habits were designed into conflict whenever possible, even within the family. Furthermore, these consequnces were worrying and awful to Fati in his teenage years and his mother. Her abilities and her vocation were in serious trouble and she was in great depression to the level that it went beyond the human limits. Many times she had been in a dilemma between two fires: either to live or not with that man who she had had very difficult years with. Each day these difficulties and hard days weighed her life. She had reached a point when everything was impossible to handle and patience had reached the limits of desperation. Very often she had thought of the possibility of breaking the imposed tradition, part of which she considered herself a victim. Now she had decided to disobey to her brothers. Now every decision was late to be taken.

She would say: "Other generations will talk about us and will judge us for living in this ugly tradition". Now her last barrier was the child she had with this man. Her life was painful. She did all the men's works, taking care of the fields, gathering grass from the meadows to feed the animals, and everything else she could. It was so difficult for her to deal with all these jobs. There was nobody there to help her. Sometimes she even felt humiliated, because the environment and time were such that women often did men's jobs. This was something not normal but the poor woman fought against the situations created by her fate. Very rare were those who understood, supported and helped her. At times, her brothers would support and help her too, especially during harvest time, threshing and mowing the lawns. They considered this as moral obligation, since they had obliged her to stay with her husband and obey the rules. The woman was so grateful and happy to the help she got by her brothers.

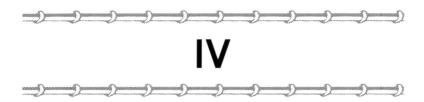

IV

The first week of February 1978 was a time of dilemma full of serious barriers and doubts. He had started studying Engineering at the University of Pristina. He had rented a so-called room, which was a space lacking even the basic necessities for living. It was just a room separated from the entire house of the owner. It was extremely humid and stingy. The ceiling was too low and completely cracked which made it difficult to walk tall and straight. In the middle of the ceiling there was a brown electric lamp. Whenever the light was on, mice would run away quickly each in their own direction. The same did different cockroaches, trying to hide away from the side walls. In the front wall there was only a small window, which instead of glass was blocked with plastic just to resist to winds and rain from outside. The room was very small. The biggest space was overtaken by a bed established over four woods upon which there was a matress filled with hay and a dirty brown torn blanket and a filthy pillow. It looked like someone had lived there and slept in that bed many years ago and it had never been cleaned. At the entrance there was a very narrow small door. There was no lock on it so it was impossible to close it completely. Opposite to the room there was a stable which had been constructed illegally. It was built by metallic walls a flat barn covered in plastic and metal too. In rainy days, the drops created a very nice harmonic music sometimes low and sometimes high from the melody reflected in the metal.

In front of the main room entrance there was a pile of fertilizer mixed with faeces of the children. The old woman each morning would take them away with a big shovel and throw them in the pile. The smell was so stingy and awful so that it could block your nise and breath. Inside the stable there was a brownish goat with its two littles and a very old dog which barked loud as if it was asking for help to be set free from the lifetime chain which had caused him bruises in the neck. In the same space, at the corner of the stable there was a big cage in which some pigeons and chickens were put together like in a prison. The owner fed them with bread gathered by leftovers around the city and gave them water through a plastic bucket which he filled from the spring nearby at the old house. Under the same roof there was a tiny toilet which smelled awfully bad. It was so small that it wasn't impossible to get in. It was used only during the day. All around this place there was an awful smell. The owner was a gypsy man, with a small body and wide chest. He coughed all the time. So much did he cough, that often the cigarette would fall down, he would bend to get it and start coughing again. He had big mustache, half yellow coloured from the strong smoking. In complexity with the face they were bigger and surpassed the dimensions of face. He was in constant moevement, coming and going out of the room carrying a plastic bag wherehe kept the food for the goat, dog, chickens and pigeons.

Fati had accepted to live in these conditions with a minimal payment, no bathroom, no water as he couldn't pay a room with normal conditions. He made the contract for a month until he finished February exams season. He passed all day long taking part in lectures and reading at the General Bookstore, but every day the idea of the shelter he was supposed to go sleeping when night came was overwhelming. But, he had no other solution. He decided to challenge the situation. In the late evenings, he entered the duvet without getting his clothes off as it was impossible to sleep in that algid. Early in the mornings he used to go in the bookstore to study. Nobody from his family knew about the bad conditions where he was living, but this was the only chance because he knew nobody could help him. He condemned himself to live there for a full month.

One late evening, while he was having dinner in the students' cafetteria, suddenly he saw his cousin, his uncle's son, who was also a student in the University of Pristina. He didn't look very available and he gavebad, direct news. All expressive he told Fati:

- Your mother is very ill and is hospitalized in the State Hospital of Skopie.

- What happened to her? - Fati asked, astonished by this unexcpected surprise.

-A brain attacks, inner bleeding, - answered the son of the uncle.

Fatal ideas came around his head. His mum's image came in front of his eyes when seeing him off that cold January morning, three weeks ago. She held him in her arms, started crying and didn't let his hands keeping them strongly tied just how a child does with his toys. She had a feeling that somebody would take him. She kissed him in the cheeks, forehead, and everywhere in the face wishing him health and good luck in his studies... As he was leaving, sheadvisedhim not to bother from the relatives, but to focus on studying and finish studies as soon as possible.

After Fati calmed down a bit, he directed to the son of his uncle:

- Is she dead!? Please, tell me, -he again directed to him repeating the question with an endless hatred!

−No, don't worry, I just came to tell you that she is not feeling well and that she will be back soon from the hospital, she has been hospitalized for four days, - he answered, tapping Fati on the shoulders. He didn't sleep all night long. His mum stood in his eyes, just like a beautifulwork of art, a vivid shade, whom he asked about the truth, but no real answer was given.....

The very next morning Fati got the first bus and went to visit his mum. During the journey, sleep deceived him repeatedly, his mind was flying everywhere and ideas were transformed into dreams. He had no support by anyone, he was desperate, physically and psychologically tired. He got off the bus sleepy. He arrivedat the hospitalin a few minutes. He got informed for his mother's room. "Room 31!"- pointed to the door the information providerat the hospital entrance. Fati wentto the right destination. He had his eyes full of tears when they finally met number 31 and he stood there immobile. He just couldn't move his feet. It was like someone had hit his knees and broken them.By intuition he had a knock at the door and feltshivers on the spine. He found his mother lying on one of the three beds. He neared to her and embraced hergently, with emotional warmth like when you hug a baby with the fear that you might hurt it.Thoughin a desperate conditionshe appeared with a sigh of extreme surprise when she realized her son was embracing her plump body. Finally, she found strength and asked:

"How come you are here my dear son, I did not want to bother and hinder you from studying"

"No, Mother, do not worry, I didn't interrupt my studies. I came to see you."

She read her son's feelings and her tears filled her eyed. He did not say anything; he did not want to bother her. She knew she was closing her eyes with regret. She begged her son to come closer again. She neared him to herself, hugged him, and tightened him so hard that didn't want to let him go. She tightened him tight with all her finalstrength; as if she wanted to take him with her and began to sob... She spoke:

-I am going beforehand. I am leaving you alone... Please, don't considerarguments with your father seriously and don't let them hurt you spiritually, even though he is the reason I'm dying! Do not oppose! Be strong! Rely on your uncles, they have promised me to help you..." Fati accepted his mother's words emotionally and wrote them in his mind!

Letting him go, she softly and quietly added: "Open the drawer of that little ummah near the bed. There were some biscuits, eat them. I can't."

Fati took and put them in his coat pocket. Then the mother took his hand, eyes full of tears, hardly speaking and said:

-My last will is your education, do not stop it! Finish it. I have always wanted you to become literate!

Fati approved bowing his head. He wasn't able to utter a single word, but tears and tears. He almost suffocated. He stayed there, holding the mother's hand till the doctors and nurses arrived informing him that the time for visits was already over. Leaving, he said:

- Mother, you will pass this over. You are a strong woman. You've been through many storms and this is just one more. You'll recover from the disease.

With a torpid smile, his words caused her more exhaustion than hope and courage. She shook her head in half-assertion and moved her fingers to greet him, releasing a profound breath from the lungs. The air came out of the mouth with difficulty. He left with his head back, went to Prishtina to take the exam that he had been preparing extremely well. Fortunately, he passed the exam excellently, but his mind still worried about his sick mother.

He went to visit her and at least to give the good news she wanted tp hear about school. Quickly he got into the hospital, directly to the room. To his surprise the bed was empty. Immediately, he feared something bad had happened. He went out to see the doctor. Asked desperately:

- Where is my mother? Where do I find my mother?

The doctor stood silent for mere moments. He thought for a while and tapped on his shoulder with the left hand. With his right hand, he expressed condolence, informing him, looking at his watch and said,

-Your mother died six hours ago!

The news was very bitter. Something strange and strong like a lightning hit his head. Sickness!He wasn't able to stand on his feet. Fell down on the floor. After a while, he recovered and said,

-I want to see my Mother's body!

He did this with perseverance. They provided him with the request. A nurse accompanied him to the mortuary, which was establiahed on the ground floor. Fati followed the nurse in the underground corridors, until she opened a huge door. At the entrance of the morgue, she opened the register and directed Fati to his mother's body. There were several corpses there. Shetold him:

-These days many other people passed away, some even younger than your mother's age, - showing the other dead bodies trying to console Fati with these words. Approaching to the body, she removed the white sheet. The dead body with eyes yet opened appeared to Fati. He murmured:

-I know the reason her eyes are half-opened. She left this world taking an immense grief with her. Her wishes and dreams were never realized...

This was the moment when Fati realisedall the regrets his mother had to take with her in the next life. He hugged her tight and spokenext to her body like an adult: -Rest in peace mother, nobody will solve all the problems of this world.

He embraced her with tears covering his cold face. Her dead body was gripped by the son who wanted to take it. He stayed for a few minutes until he told all the unspoken words he hadn't been able to tell her alive. He closed her eyes with the greatest care by convincing himself with the reality he faced and said:

-Farewell my dearest mother for the last time!

When they got out of the mother's body, he turned his head back and set off in the wrong direction until he found the exit door. He whispered: - Good bye, my lovely mother, you went away without enjoying the 43rd spring! How hard it is to say goodbye to mother forever.

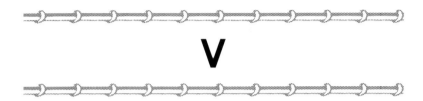

V

Now Fati had to go through great difficulties and to take responsibilities. The barrier in front of him seemed like an impermanent iron curtain with harsh conditions. Closed paths without horizons appeared in front of him. It was very obvious that he was trying to behave as he should in this interment ceremonial moment before the people who were watching him and that was contrary to the concern expressed in his eyes, because everyone's focus was on him. He was communicating with his eyes, looking at his mum like a work of art with his mind, keeping the eyes concentrated on his mother's coffin.

at this very moment everything was about his mother and no circumstance would interefere crucial bond. He owned the entire conscience and obedience to stand face to face to her at these final moments. His soul and heart were aching and burning, though he felt frozen like a bird inside the prison cage. Gloomy clouds announced whirling storms from up the sky, frozen bushes.

The windblew harshely and scattered streams of snow. Empty branches of the trees shivered like scared of what they were witnessing. From the frozen points, their light kicks fell to thousands of slopes. A loud noise emerged from the powerful wind. The body spontaneously shivered from the cold and he felt the continuous sobbing that responded to the next big sobbing associated with the hot tears flowing through the frozen cheeks. This idea killed his consciouness at the most thrilling moment of pain as he stood at the entrance of the Mosque in front of the coffin placed on a flat stone raised half a meter from the ground that was especially designed for this purpose.

There, the dead body of his mother, covered in a white sheet, was lying like a horizontal statue. They were preparing to put it inside the tomb opened by the young volunteer boys of the neighborhood. Among them was also Uncle Hajdari, a master and punctual artist on everything he did. He was also a good mason. She had asked him to open the tomb with great mastery, so he was digging the ground with some young men until it was opened in the middle of the cemetery of the village where she would be buried. At the ceremony of the congregation, they were praying and praying for the deceased inside the village mosque. His thoughts were disturbed by the strong wind that whistled and moved the white sheet over the mother's carcass. The uninterrupted movement of the white sheet by the strong wind almost indicated that the woman surrendered this world peacefully and lost the battle with life.

As she lied inside the coffin, the words of the deceased came to his mind, her last will before she passed away.

She advised him to do his best not to abandon his education and to continue regardless the sacrifices and challenges he would face as this was the last idea and will, that stands as a dome over her closed eyes. She often said: "You must have special strength to start from scratch because mine has exhausted as soon as I will close my eyes forever."

Her desire was education, and only education at the right moment. Intellectual work was the joy her son could gift her. This was the last will that she had addressed with convincing words. These feelings made Fati feel proud for having sworn speechless in front of the dead body that he would accomplish her message to the end. She had lived in times of great crises, fierce confrontations. Even though she had experienced these crises, in the outer appearance she seemed calm and self-contained. Basically, she had a fiery temperament...

Fati was lost. He was losing logic at the time. His eyelids became dark like coal, even though they were hidden under the eyebrows. They were ready to get in flames and there was nothing that could extinguish this lava that was emerging from the inner volcano. He talked to the mother's body from the inner side, with the last words she had told him and he tried to repeat them again before putting her in the soil. The eyes embedded on the dead body harassed spiritual moments. He remembered that her life finished so early very painfully, that is why she left many messages. At the last moments of her life, she had spoken to him with regret, because she was convinced that she was leaving this life and knew that she was leaving behind the challenges that Fati had to face in his life. She had said him:

- You now have more and more responsibilities.

Fati recalled her words and everything he had seen, even though he was still young, to understand everything she had said. The time she left, which she had felt was corresponding to many other things that she didn't say. She was convinced that in the unsafe hands she was leaving all those griefs to the one who beforehand brought all the crap to the calamity of life.

He knew that she had suffered a lot from that hand and thus closed the short chapter of life with words stuck in his throat and opened eyes without realizing her dreams. When he was in bed often she got up, grited her teeth in the face of pain, but did not complain. How come that she didn't complain?! Because there was no one to whom she could. She escaped forever with a hocked smile. Until the last minute of life, she did not leave the conversation and conseil for the children she was leaving in God's safe hands. Fati had often heard saying:

-O God! We are in your hands. Please mercy us!

This human was loved by wood and stone …

In front of him stood Lemi, the first cousin of Fati as a static honor guard, staggered as a bronze statue. He hadsome tiny bubbles of sweat in his forehead, and his feet were shaking from the knees in the cold.

Thoughts were interrupted by the sound of the jammed shoe-shaping sound coming out of the mosque. This noise was special and it was devised by the crowd toward a certain place. They were all set off and four people caught the coffin by raising it on their shoulders. Fati felt as if she was abducted with violence and cut off his thoughts with a knife. The caravan began to squeeze the seven snakes and walk through the main street of the neighborhood.

Fati's tears were clearly defined in his pale face; they almost passed in the other side of the chapter, by avoiding the thoughts that came over forty minutes standing before the coffin. He joined the caravan and cried, sobbed like a child. Someone threw his arm to comfort him. It was an old man.Seeing the tears that came out of his eyes as a volcano that had burst from inside his body, he said, tightening his shoulders:

-Don't worry, my mother also died when I was little I don't even remember her. While you were delighted with the mother's scent. All of us who have come, one by one will go there, because this is the truest and safest way we are unable overcome.

Fati didn't find comfort in these words, on the contrary, these strange words he had not heard before, careless to who said them, made his pain stronger. Tears flowed from his eyes like streams of river. Someone said, "Cry as much as you can for your mother, don't be ashamed to cry for her, I still cry for my mother I have never seen, I never felt my mother's scent! She gave me birth and went to the eternal world!"

Fati paid no attention to the comforting and comparative words, he felt the same misery. The caravan walked without stopping. People ran as much as they could to carry the funeral with the body of the deceased to earn as much rewards, that's what the Imam said when they left the mosque.

-The more you carry the coffin on your shoulders with the body of the dead and the more you throw soil on it with shovels or hands on the grave of the dead, the more you will get thanks from the Lord or as they say in the language of the religion, Rewards. The cortege went on his way to the tomb. No one spoke. You could only hear the hasty steps while carrying the funeral on each other's shoulders, so everyone had the opportunity to do this "rewarding" and most of the cases were confused by slipping out of the humidity of the snow that had dampened the ground there. Even tired snuffers, as soon as the funeral was put inside the tombstones, rushed hurriedly to the courtyard until they left the funeral near the open tomb. Everything was done as if it had been previously planned. The village Imam just made a sign and orders were executed.

The dead body wrapped with a white cloth is pulled out of the coffin from the close family with the utmost care and let off inside the grave. Then the half-turn-boards were placed for forty-five stairs. The Imam once again addressed to the audience by explaining that the more they would throw soil on the tomb the more rewards they would get. Fati's uncle first threw a fist of soil to the tomb of his dead sister and he came close to fati. He said in his ear: -you should do something similar, throw soil inside the tomb! He refused to do something like that in his mother's body and pulled back. His uncle again gave the orderly sign to act.

He realized that the world also speaks through gestures, and the command had to be implemented. With the greatest climax approaching close to the soil with huge cubes coming out of the pit of the tomb and whispering: "Forgive me, Mother, that without asking you I am covering you with soil and making it heavy!" Without speaking at all, something came into his mind while throwing the fist filled with soil he stammered:

-May this soil be easy to your body!

He went to the others. His hands were shaking. Something from the inside stirred him up and, instead of an answer; the tears came to his cheeks and poured inside the tomb. He felt that his mother felt the weight of the pain she took with her. Someone pulled him from behind advising him not to worry. He obeyed and apologized to those near him. Fati was watching by accompanying the attendees who made it fast, all ordered to use the shovel in order to cover the tomb.

He went out of box with his ideas, and he couldn't stand those that were throwing soil on his mother's grave. Now Fati couldn't resist the internal volcano that annoyed him.

He was now convinced that his mother left forever entering on the black ground. His tears came out like a stream. He had no power, his feet and hands were weak and unintentionally he fell down. Someone ran and raised him up, but he couldn't stand at his feet. Someone cried out to bring some water, but there was no water. There was only one container that was brought to moisten the tomb and this water was not preferable to be used for other things. Someone found some snow and put it in the chest.

The cold and damp snow, madehim conscious so he gave a sign that he was okay and thanked them. He apologized for the situation created. After a pottery was created from the dust on the grave, someone took care for everything to be done according to the traditions. He placed in the position above a stick that was equal to the length of the deceased, took a container of water, bathed the rod at the top of the grave, and at the head on the soft soil, put a chalkboard in the vertical A form of a curse, without epitaph as a sign to know whose subject is the tomb.

The earth was moistened by the sleet. It was raining cats and dogs! People started opening umbrellas half destroyed by the wind. Now the Imam sang *TALLEM* and finally asked people present, by repeating three times:

-Do you make it hallall? The participants repeated after him for three times in row:

-Hallall! Hallall! Hallall!

The Imam ordered to sit down, pray and sing for the soul of the deceased. They all sat down. The Imam firstsang verses from Glorious Quran. Silence reigned, and the voices of the Imam were barely audible to the sound of the wind and the crunches of the magpie and the black ravens flying around the cemetery surroundings. With their crunches, they broke the mortal silence. He had a much enriched vocabulary. It seemed like the moon, the sun, earth atmosphere and the Glorious God were in a dialogue with one another. Some elders also sang some verses. After the burial ceremony was over, the Imam got up. All stood up after him, getting rid of the numbness from feet. The Imam ordered the members of the deceased's family to rank a little further and the attendees to approach. They would express their condolescence before they went to their homes. Relatives, friends, and other people from other villages took their directions like wombs appearing through the trees' leaves to console. Most of them embraced Fati expressing sincere words of condolence. Apparently, they all understood the pain he felt.

Fati didn't feel well. It was scorching hot, poor him, what could he say? He was more than smashing. His face darkened, and traces of tears left marks on his face. He wasn't there physically even though people consoled him sincerely. He looked aroundto the other and thought," All them first got sick and then died. Who knows how many nursing mothers and babies are covered with this soil. This is terrible," he said to himself. "Oh God, why did you take my mother I loved and loved me so much? Why didn't you take me?"

Logic betrayed him here. Surely the mother hadprayed God beforehand. Maybe she had said: "Take me first, and do not let me see my child die before me!"

He got angry. He frowned. His hair on the forehead shook. He no longer liked the logic. It was useless to be persuaded by anyone. His eyes darkened. He felt dizzy and his blood pressure lowered. He was squinting in his face, almost fainting. Others did not notice his spiritual insight. Reluctantly, he didn't keep on his feet and fell down. His cousins, Lema and Mala, helped him; they quickly stood up and set him in the middle, holding both sideways.

Once he woke up and felt strong. He wanted to be let to walk alone. They came home, but all the ideas that were accumulated on their heads were desperate and didn't let them go. Lema and Mala, his first cousins and peers did not leave him alone in those difficult moments. Misery was immense, even in moments of joy that were inseparable in everyday life. In such situation, he needed someone to be close to him. The presence of Lema and Mala gave him spiritual strength relieving the pain.

The uncle who was making decisions and trying to convince the others for their realization, seeing Fati who was fully immersed in the basin of pain approached kindly. He sat down in front of him at the same height and stretched out his hand, holding it apart, until he finished the words and, with his other hand, tapped him on his head and shoulder murmuring:

-Be strong and don't shed tears for your mother, because tears will burden her soul and death is part of life and we must accept it as an unstoppable and inevitable process. Here you have the grandfather, grandmother great grandfather, and great grandmother and others from our family, let's not go any further in our kinship and friendship.

This is how his uncle spoke to him, sitting in the same position in front of Fati, until someone from the corridor's open door called him out. He stood up letting one hand, and by removing the other hand from his head. In silence, Fati accepted everything. As soon as the uncle left, he took all Fati's words with him. He weepedscreaming, coughing with a sting that bothered him as a result of the cold he took when he was at the cemetery.

Lema and Mala, spontaneously commanded by the spiritual feelings they felt for Fati, threw their arms on his shoulders, embracing and supporting him as a sign of comfort. He wasn't interested in comfort. His mind was blurred, and everything was obscure in his sight. He couldn't get out of his skin. He was sluggish and wasn't hungry at all. Even though they approached him to eat some "hallvë" for the sake of the deceased, he did not accept it. Hallva was specially prepared according to the tradition. Doing this gesture, he didn't want to accept the reality that his mother was dead. Even though the attitude of the attendees was very human, he seemed different because his brain was working differently. His image was sad. He considered death the most unfair judge, because it took his mother at the very best age in a golden part of her life, just 43 years.

"I don't deserve such a loss, such a cruel and severe punishment. I don't know how to describe the portrait of a person that I loved and loved me so much. This is not an easy thing "- this is how Fati commented to himself this event. Thoughts were interrupted by his aunt, his mother's sister with tears in her eyes, she careesed and kissed his forehead. She said these comforting words to Fati and herself: "We have to agree with the God's commands and not grieve that we lost, but thank him for what we had so precious. God loved her and took her with him." Then he surrendered to physical and psychological fatigue. Sleep came along with the night, grabbing him, in small tricks and sent him away from allterrible ideas. A voice appeared in the shape of his mother, asking him by hand to get closer. Caressing her head, she advised:

-Whatever your situation, and spiritual condition is, never get tired of looking out of the sky! Pray, believe, and the Lord will do miracles for you!

He wasn't calm even asleep. Some ghosts came around him that had appeared during the day too. Some old and dull pictures got in front of his eyes. He was in delirium. His sleep was disturbed after every worry and frightening dream. His mother's face looked too big out of the sky as if she was waving: "Come, come here, paradise is here!"

She spoke these words and escaped hiding behind the dense clouds.

In the morning, he got up with clearer ideas and everything seemed normal and acceptable to what had happened. Sleep proved to be a successful action, though with a sense of emptiness in the soul. He felt the brain to be relaxed. With his back hand, he wiped sweat on his forehead and around his neck. Worry was reduced. He went straight to the toilet. The image that came out in the mirror didn't fit his identity. But he was silent and kept calm, even though his brain came back with memories back as in a video recorder. Everything appeared in front of his eyes, from yesterday and back in time bringing sequences of memories. He didn't say a word and his eyes were damp.

They shone sparkling when recalled the most beautiful days they had spent together during his childhood. He recalled some episodes of happiness, but now this happiness was vanished by this last terrible episode of her loss.

Once the veil of this idea came out, he went back to the mirror, cleaned his face slightly, brushed his hair, and noticed he still had haunted eyes. His knees shook a bit as if he had been drunk. He was still under her influence. He wanted to eat something, he also asked for hallva and a glass of milk. After having breakfast, he felt better and realised now he could accept the reality. He was now completely awakened and became aware of the reality, that he should continue his normal life.

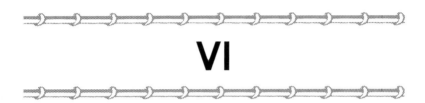

VI

Since early in the morning the uncles (from mother and father sides) consulted for the organization of the reception of people who were expected to come for condolences. They assigned some young men giving duties who would look after some of the ceremony services. Someone would look after drinks, someone accompany guests, at least to serve them an apple or orange juice and refreshments of coca-cola and Schweppes, still water or mineral water. Some young people were assigned to make the reception outside the yard and guide the people to the reception room at uncle's home.

It was decided that during lunchtime all the participants would eat "bread" (meaning lunch) in the next room where the table was set. According to the tradition, the family of the dead doesn't set tables and doesn't cook for three days, therefore, three neighbours were offered as volunteers. They confirmed that they would bring food for the participants for the first three days. This was done by the first three neighbors until the third day. People came for condolesence and this made Fati strong and proud. The big room started getting crowded. They came and went as soon as the other group of people came. His uncles were present since morning and received condelescence with sympathy and sincerity. They stood cross legged in the lower corner of the room and talked with the guests. On the first day, many people came and there wasn't enough space in the room so they only said comforting words and they stood up slowly to leave space to the next group. There were people coming until late afternoon.

This gave a positive impression to Fati who felt proud of these people honoring the family with these comforting visits. Next night he slept better than the night before. The same happened the next day. People came and went in crowds. He thought to write the names of visitors and took a notebook. He did this secretly, when people went. He entered the other room and wrote the names of people coming and going not stopping. There were endless crowds of people. Almost everyone felt an obligation. The young people who were assigned to do the services accomplished them very well. The first one counted the number of comers and the other filled the glasses with juice. The third served the tray with filled glasses and the other gave out cigarettes. The other was standing like a pipe on his feet, and quickly lit the cigarette to those that were holding in the hand.

Fati's uncle stood in front of them, waiting for people who comforted about his youngest sister. With a man's prudence, he talked and thanked them one by one. Until the third day the organization went well according to the arrangements. Meals were set by neighbours. After a week of reception people still arrived in groups. At the top of the column stood the oldest, leading the column just like a lamb leading the sheep. As soon as they sat, he got the word and expressed condolence to the family. They usually spoke good words about the deceased proving that she was really a good person, because she was a decisive person always helping and supporting others.

At the time when less people arrived, they drank coffee, as there was time and space for reception. During this time, they were talking about the deceased and taken as an example to others. This gave Fati pride. These good words made him feel comfortable and proud. It was great moral support. These words gave him the conviction in the words of the deceased who had told him before she left forever. So, the good words and good acts are left after life. Even the stars as they shine, one day they fall as meteors. Thus, in this world everyone is designed to be born and dead. The shorter the life is, the much more painful it becomes. Fati was concerned about the destiny of his mother and about the fact that she didn't leave longer. If she had the possibility to be still alive, he would learn many more lessons from her... But, look, she fled like a tree trunk. She crashed and fell. Branches flew in the air. However, her orientation will not disappoint him and life will guide him related to the environment that would surround it without going out of the box.

The Imam of the village was everyday present when people came to visit. On the fifth day, after coming from the lunch prayer, he reminded his family that on the seventh day they had to make a "Qilime" (dinner) for the seventh day of her death. This was accepted and confirmed by the uncle too.

"Bread should be given for the soul of the dead", the Imam said.

The next day, dinner preparations began for the reverence and respect of the soul of the deceased. In addition to family members, the neighbors also committed to contribute in honor and respect for the soul of the deceased. Many people were invited. After verifying the number of guests that was 60, they started preparing four large tables with 16 people each.

Later theQilima procedure started. After it, the round sofas were set two into two rooms.

VII

According to the tradition, the time of condolence was now over. Now more difficult days were to come for the orphan children of the family. The absence and nostalgia for the mother increased day by day. Fati was in big problems. He needed his father's help and attention. He tried to talk to him but it was useless. The father had different way of thinking and he was convinced that the child could never be braver and smarter than the father. Thus, he was careless to any of the complaints of the son. Moreover he did the opposite of what his son wanted or asked for. Due to bad management the economic situation was going further down. The father wanted to get married for a second time. This was acceptable for Fati and he welcomed the idea. Due to bad management of the incomes the economic situation was going down and down. The father needed to get married for a second time as, according to him, thiswould improve the physical and psychological situation inside the family, though the pain for the lost mother just a few weeks ago was still fresh. Finally the father announced that he thought of getting married. This was reasonable. To the children this would be a relief, because they needed the care and attention of someone to be near them...... However, it wasn't so easy to get married again as the idea was obstacled by his children, and nobody would allow giving a young lady for marriage to an old man with children. This was the reason why he was being refused, and getting nervous, thus rebelling in front of his children telling them they were the reason he couldn't get married. There was a total chaos inside the family. The orphan children neededfinancial and emotional support, which was lacking at the time. The biggest problem was the oldest son, Fati. A cousin of him who wanted to do matching for the marriage had told Fati that actually, he was the only problem. He had clearly said to him that the supposed woman had replied she couldn't get married to someone who had a boy. She could handle the girls, as one day they would get married and would leave home, but with the boy it was a completely different story. The father started to hate Fati to that point that it was impossible for him to recognize him as his own son. He saw Fati as a clear obstacle impossible to get through.

The hate for his son was stronger and deeper every day. Thus he started to torture him and to make his life unbearable.

Fati had no one to complain. Who would believe that he was being tortured by his father?! This was absurd and unacceptable. Fati wasn't calm! He recalled the words of his mother asking him to not contradict, because there was no chance for him to win. These ideas, thoughts and behaviours accompanied him everywhere, and very often he tried to converse with himself, like a monologue: "What should I do?!"

One late night, lying in bed, thinking loud about a way to solve the situation, he fell in deep sleep. Dreams sent him to what he feared the most. All his friends playing and running with joy, whereas he, out of any activities, trying to jump in a deep endless abyss. He tried to commit suicide and there was this inner voice ordering to do it as quickly as possible and to set his father free and make possible the idea of marriage. It was his father's voice, who stared at him from inside the window, waving and ordering him to jump. During his jumping the appalling scream woke him up and helped him to quieten down until he was convinced that it was just a dream.

So scared and sad he couldn't sleep any longer. It took him long to understand and convince himself that it was just a dream. Tired from insomnia, only sometime the very early morning did he manage to sleep. Sleep sent him to a new dream.

The father was now wearing solemn clothes, with a very nice blue coat, beautifully matched with the rest of the outfit. He kept the passport proudly in his hand. It was night, not dawn yet but he shone from the brightness of his clothes. He was about to leave home and to go somewhere abroad. He put the money in a big ko'pher which he barely pulled. He was leaving town as someone had promised to match him with a beautiful young lady. Fati with the courage of a real man, but with his voice trembling from fear had gone in front of the strings trying to block him. His heart was broken, it hurt more than the physical violence he had been going through all over his body. Standing tall and strong in front of his father he said repeatedly:

-Kill me before you get out of this door. Kill me, father, before you abandon us!

In the end he fell down, exhausted begging and crying:

-Father, where are you going like this? How are you leaving us? In such conditions?

He didn't listen to the voice and begging of his son, who asked to impede his father on any condition. The father was so angry and didn't care about the son's words. His face was reddish and he finally said:

-I don't intend to be a widow all my life.

He took a knife out of his pocket. He lost every parental and human feeling. He threatened the son with life if he didn't let him pass and shouted with the knife on the son's chest:

-Let me go! Let me go! There is no one in this world that can stop me, and you are trying to do it.

At this very moment he went fast towards his son. Fati, feeling strong and brave directed his chest towards him:

-You better kill me before you leave home!

Before the father could kill him with the knife, Fati woke up. He found himself sobbing under the pillow. He couldn't breathe. In mere minutes he got released, thanking God that it had been just a bad dream.

Fati kept on dreaming such awful dreams every day. There was no one he could complain about this. One day he thought of discussing the problem with the Imam of the village. He convinced the priest that there was no other choice but comitting a scandal of tragical consequences. The imam considered these troubles of Fati as a very serious issue. After learning the truth he got convinced of what he could do and intervened advising him to get out of this tragedy. One day, the imam decided to get inside Fati's house together with his counsellor. They had a closed-door conversation together with Fati's father. They discussed and judged all the facts and reality. They understood that the decision was irrevocable. This was really a difficult decision but that was the truth. They couldn't convince him so they left desperate from his disobedience. He even accused them as uninvited in his house. He didn't feel good for the fact that they protected the son he constantly accused as wrong and offensive.

The following day, the imam invited Fati and together with the counsellors went to the chairman of the village. In the big room where he stood there were three cousins, and the two uncles. He was impressed by the people who were there listened attentively and carefully to what Fati was telling to all of them. They took a decision which was, to send Fati somewhere far from his house and to find a shelter for him at his uncle's house, convinced that in such way things would improve. They announced his father for this who accepted the solution introduced from these people. He agreed to send his son to his uncle. The uncle too had been informed from his nephew that after his mother's death, things weren't going properly.

Fati accepted dialogue instead of violence, because he had no other choice. This was the least awful choice. The following day he went to his uncle's. The uncle was quite interested to once more listen to the words of his nephew in order to make sure all his doubts were true. He stood legs-crossed in the middle of the room and felt very embarrased to what Fati confessed. Moving his hand on the head he took the hat off and said: -Poor you my son!

He scratched his head and tears filled his eyes. He responded to the nephew in a supportive way:

-My dear nephew, stay here in my house. I understand the situation because that man did the worst to my sister and made her life impossible at a very early age and I suppose he will do the same with you.

The boy apologised to his uncle for having put him into trouble.

He recommended him not to return home for some days, until they found a solution.

In this situation, the boy found consolation and started feeling much better.

On the other hand, the father, having confirmed that the son would not return home anymore, announced the matcher that he could fulfill the condition asked by the family of his future wife.

"My son has left house forever! Nowwe can continue with the marriage!" were his words.

When this was verified and confirmed the wife came home. A few days later the uncle came up with an idea of sending the nephew near his sons in Switzerland. He talked to them and asked them to find a job for his son. This was very quickly realized, as, not only did he help his siblings, but his health condition changed together with the social situation as well.

VIII

A year after getting his passport, Fati was made redudant at his job in Switzerland. He needed to sumbit the MilitaryService then he could get the passport and continue working. This was a condition placed bythe state and was irrevocable. He absolutely had to complete it in order to carry on with his job.

With the interference of his uncle he managed to commit in the MilitaryService in ex-Yougoslavian Army. He went in the military service of Montenegro, the country of massacres commited to more than 4600 Albanians in the famous Tivar.

The time when Fati served in the Yugoslavic Army was extremely difficult for Albanians, because they were victims of the SerboSlavic chauvinism. The Albanian soldiers from the occupied areas of Yugoslavia were tortured, sentenced of many years imprisonment without true facts of their imprisonment and they were killed, and then given the diagnosis of commiting suicide. Everything ended there; there was no accusation, no judgement. The victim was blamed and accused as terrorist, irredentistand deserter or tending to grab any weapon and kill any Serbian soldier or any other nationality. The contrivance of the murder was done saying that the soldier of the other nationality needed to self-defendso he ended up killing the Albanian soldier. This was the etiquette given to the Albanian soldiers. Fati couldn't be different.Badluck chased him along the period he served in thisinfamous army.

In a total lack of truths and facts, he was accused of being an irrendentist and being caught while listening to KukësiRadio and watching the Albanian National Television. Due these shameful accusations the chief of the military contentment in Tivar, the MontenegrianLieutenant VujoviçVelko accused and brought him in front of the battalionin the military contentment to witness that, supposingly, he was irredentist and enemy of the Yugoslavic Army forces interested in the Great Albania and other territories inhabited with Albanians in the Yugoslavic lands. This took place in order for anyone to know that if something happened it would be because of him as traidor and deserter of the Yugoslavian Army. The case was announced as a crime committed against the Brotherhood Joining of the residents living in Yugoslavia. This was inscenation of the witch hunting having prepared the thorough destruction of what had been built in other lands inhabited by Albanians, not choosing ways and methods. This started from persons, intelectuals, to JudiciarySystem members such as lawyers, and employeed of the state institutions civil and military. Such was the case of Fati. He was brought there to witness the inscenation created by Colonel Vujoviç Velko. This anti-Albanian tried with what he could to carry out a fake event in front of the battalion with a declaration in which he was announced irredentist and separatist. Fati stood in front of the battalion, innocent and unhappy.

He recalled his grandfather saying:

"You never know who the enemy is. They are treacherous. Be careful!They fake stories in order to reach high and awarding positions. In different times the military chiefs have committed cruel crimes, murders and massacres to young Albanian sons, and they lost their traces accusing the very same people of terrrorism and separatism. They used various methods for execution. He recalled the High Grade Commissary Milladin Popoviqi who asked Enver Hoxha, on behalf of Yugoslavian Communist Party, to clean and execute the whole terrain from the ballists and chauvinists and armed bands. They created the opportunity to train Albanian-speaking spies and enter Kosovo or Metohi (the Yugoslavic term referred to Kosovo) and to act energetically and merciless. Thus, when this category of enemies was discovered they were immediately executed from the communist regime. Properties and possessions were taken away from their relatives; those who remained alive emigrated mainly in Turkey, Europe America until farAustralia. After the completion of all these orders especially in Kosovo, Macedonia, Montenegro and Preseva the entire wealth of the killed Albanians was smuggledand given to the Serbian-Montenegrin Colonists according to the directions of the National Comittee and Yugoslavic Communist Party.

These memories were interrupted by the loud voice of the lieutenant who spoke without proofs or facts. For three days he was questioned by two officers and a translator. It was interesting the way they behaved. They were quite correct and put no pressure to him. Fati was clear in his answers and he used to talk to them in a very comfortable and precise way. He put his right hand somewhere between the eyebrow and the eye, on the right part of face and would answer: "Yes Sir!"

Vujovic was a tall man, old enough to be active in the military service but still very aggressive. He talked loud and this was kind of scary for the people around him. However his attitude didn't scare Fati at all. He was quite confident in his statements and reactions.

The man had long heavy mustache covering the upper lips. He had dirty yellow teeth because of being a regular smoker. Fati read in his eyes a big hate towards the Albanians, who at the time were a quite significant number conquered by Yugoslavia.

These were times when the Albanian soldiers had to be very careful to what they said to the military forces because they could be under provocations at any time. Fati thought about the power of words. In the end it was all about words. Thet created society, culture, development, agreement, listening and good-manners. So, he was conscious that this would be his solution so he decided to behave well and to speak as well as possible. He knew he had to survive to the provocations he had to go through.

He knew as well that even little babies would be part of such provocations and reprisals, not only him. In all military contentments there were Albanians failing to resist and falling into Serbian traps. The issue of each person's personal future was questioned. They tried to kill people so that the project finished as soon as possible. If a young unmarried boy was killed an entire future family was killed too.

In his office Vujovic spoke loud and asked fro Fati's answers. But what could Fati say?! He had no answers! He asked about the Albanian issue, the Albanian school, the Albanian people and to one point he rotates 180 grades, opens the door of the board and takes out a fire gun, nears to Fati and puts the gun just in front of his mouth and says:

-Listen, only this works best for you and all your people! If you don't answer I'll kill you with this, do you hear?!

He stepped back and offended Fati in national and spiritual basis.

-You think that you will kill our soldiers with your weapons, don't you?!

I am asking you, how many times have you tried to pass the border?

-I have never tried, sir!

-Have you read "Titistët" of Enver Hoxha?

-No,-he said.

-Are you here willing to serve the APJ?

-Yes.

-Why are you here to serve, to learn how to kill Yugoslavic soldiers?

He thought a little bit longer and answered to that man dressed in a long coat who anytime created the image of a mechanical statue at any oh his moves.

-I have come and sworn in front of the national flag to fulfill and commit to any obligation or duty as a citizen of this country, to serve for my sacred family that you are offending, to serve the people of my country and to be able to protect my country. He said this in a rush, nervous but courageous too. Vujoviçgave the impression that he wasn't attentively listening and continued with other questions and Fati continued with other replies.

-Which is your country?

-Yugoslavia, sir.

-Mention seven heroes of the National Liberal War.

- Emin Duraku, Boro Vukmiroviq, Ramiz Sadiku, Milladin Popoviqi, Fadil Hoxha, Mustafa Bakijadhe Dushan Mugosha.He stressed out these names on purpose because Vujoviçknew that some of them had been politicans and military emissars in Albania.

-Is it true that you have been watchingNAT (National Albanian Television) have listened to Kukësi Radio?

-Yes comarade, it is true.

When he got this answer he stepped back, took a wooden chair, leaned it next to him and approached it to his body. He put one foot over the chair and his forearm over the knee. He leaned on his chin and coughed directing to Fati as a winner.

-Now we are at the point where I wanted us to be. Why do you watch such programs in Albanian? Do you know it is forbidden by law? - He asked.

-Yes I know but all of us the soldiers when we had free time we have watched it, we have played cards, chess, someone reads and someone writes, someone talks to the others and someone listens to the radio, someone else watches television and movies in different channels, be them italian, bulgarian, albanian and yugoslavian. We have done this for entertainment satisfying our needs, approaching to each other and creating an atmosphere of happiness, forgetting about the worries of life, - Fati declared.

-What about Kukës Radio, do you listen to it?

-I have listened to it, but now I don't anymore, because this is forbidden too.

-What attracts you more in NAT and Kukësi Radio?

-The music, comarade.

-So. Albania lies in your heart? - was the next provocative question

-No,-he replied.

-Why not? Albania is your country.

-This is my country. This is where my grandparents and I were born and here is where I will live.

At that moment he pointed to the floor, stating what he previously said. Albania is your country, - he pointed the southern part.

-Why are you lying? -the lieutenant interrupted. This is not your country. Albania, that is your country,-he pointed the south taking the leg away from the chair, raising the voice pointed to the direction of Albania. Fati had this inner feeling like a volcanoe and told him: "Yes, yes Albania is my country!" - But he didn't say that because it was prohibited. And then his thoughts were interrupted by the loud voice if Vujoviç.

-One day, you will be all sent there! He coughed. He could hardly speak. He directed to Fati.

-What do you reccomend to your co-nationalists related to the service in this strong military force armata of the region? Fati answered ironically:

-I suggest they should be proud for having vowed this country where the rights and freedoms of all people and all countries are respected. To fulfill all their duties and respect the military rules, not to ofend others in national basis because it is difficult to overcome when someone in a higher position offends you in such basis.

Vujoviçinterrupted emotionally losing control and paled in his face protesting in the most unhuman way and raised his voice louder, neared to Fati and pushed him to the wall, got him in his jacket and fiercely told him the worst of words:

-Shut up! Are you trying to do phylosophy here?! Get the hell out of here and come tomorrow to take part in the report and don't forget to bring information of all your damn Albanians that are in this contentment, about what they have said per each. But be careful! Don't you dare to lie! We do have information and facts about everything you have talked with your Albanians.

-Yes sir, I will serve my community! - Fati said and left as a real winner to go to the prison room accompagnied by the guard. He had a feeling that something bad was about to happen that night. He didn't sleep all night. He had this feeling of insecurity. The very next morning, he is invited by the mayor of First Grade who was present in the meeting he had together with the lieutenant in his office. They announced Fati that he would be transferred in the contentment with other soldiers and the whole staff, sentenced and prosecuted starting from the simplest soldier to the highest military grade.

-I think it will be better for you there, though the whole garnizon has been sentenced. - said the mayor of First Grade accompanying him to the door and apologising for the inconveniences. He tried to comfort Fati apologising once more for not being able to help him, but this was the least bad aspect. This news pleased Fati though he didn't know what he should expect in that new contentment with military people been sentenced. Now he was in the right direction, at least this is what he thought. All the way from Tivar to Zagreb he thought about all these things. And his feelings resulted to be true. The next part of the military service that he passed in the contentment of military sentenced, somewhere in Vojvodinë he had a better time than in the one of Tivar. There he encountered people who had been sentenced from the Yugoslavian Army and 70% of them were of Albanian nationality, starting from the simple soldier to the highest grades. Fati needed some time to adapt the situation and conditions. Later he understood that his arrival here had been the only way for him to escape the physical execution the lieutenant Vujoviç had threatened him.

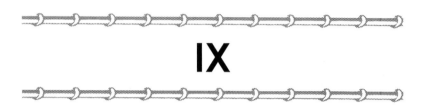

IX

After the one-year military service Fati called his "ex-boss", that's how he called the employer. He said he was ready to work in case there was any job offered by part of the employer. The boss offered to provide him with a permanent job. Going back to Switzerland he managed to regulate his financial situation and to help his family as well, his brothers, and sistersand building a house for his younger sisters. Moreover he put some money aside for his education. Things were going fine. Fati was very grateful for his well being to the employer Mr. Takmak who was a 65 year-old man, bachelor.

He lived just with the memories of his youth gone away. He had some of his friends with whom he communicated in silence with a mysterious language. He only sang his songs of the very famous swiss singer Appanzell loudly, without being interrupted by anyone else.

Fati went to University while still working in Switzerland. He completed his studies successfully. Though he started building a new house he was still impeded by his father, due to the fact that he thought that this would make Fati return to the village.

Found insuch situation Fati leaves the village again, this time because of his father's pressure and spiritually broken.

After his graduation Fati moves to the capital, gets employed as a teacher, he gets married and creates his own family. Despite all the difficulties, he finally starts having a positive relationship with his father though there still was the biggest barrier, his step-mother, who constantly impeded them two meeting and talking to each other.

Fati never returned to his hometown. However, he was supportive to his father and siblings to what he could.

 SECOND PART

Plan for Eviction

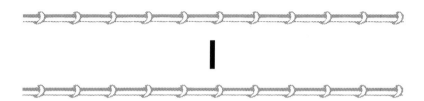

I

Imam Ymer Efendi was the son of the former Imam of the village in the suburbs. He was a very good communicator and very close to the people and environment around. He spoke soft and sweet. He was the type of person who would speak softly even to the animals, as he considered them as creatures of God which needed love and respect. Thus he would bless them with nice words any time he could. Due to his good-behaviour, devotion to his profession based on the rules of the sacred book The Glorious Quran. He was addressed to as the most respectful man in the village and further. With his manners, image, ideals, spiritual ability and his generous heart he made these qualities more persuasive to the eyes of people around. He was very talented. He was a great man. He enhanced his values. He had strong positive aspects. His hobby was work. He worked to provide food and clothes for his family not just to earn money, because this world is a mystery, life is short and it's atrick, thus it may very quicklyend. We are expected to work for the next world and the eternal life.

Children were very happy any time they met the imam in the streets or somewhere else. He gave them sweets which he kept in his pocket and whenever he saw them he would provide them with these sweets or candies. The children now thought that they were part of his body. Anytime he met the children, alone or in groups he would put his hand in the pocket and take out the candies smiling and asking them to approach. He spoke to them very softly, caressed their heads and wished joy ans hapiness to everyone. Those he didn't know he asked about their names and father's name. Sometimes he would even make predictions about the family of the child related to the physionomy of the child itself.

Often their mothers, when children did something wrong at home they would ask to be quiet and not to make mistakes otherwise the imam wouldn't give them sweets.

He had inhereted this profession by his father who had asked him to transmit such profession to all other generations. His grandfather was well known as one of the first imams and very famous in the area and a very influencing man. He was educated in Istanbul and was the most literate man of the region. His job as an imam had made big influence on the spread of the Muslim religion in these parts of the country. His project had been a strong point to attract the investors of the Turkish government. In the lands of Vakef he had built the mosque of the village with high minarees accompanied by two cherifs which was the first one of this kind in the village. A pashá from Turkey had invested on this, so it was called the "Mosque of the Pashá". Apparently, he didn't want to show off with his name, because he considered this as a work in the name of God and religious. Under the same barn, he had built a facility for the necessities of the time such as: a Mejtepwhere the children of the village learned elementary reading through the Arabic alphabet from the Glorious Quran. Then the hamam, a small kitchen and a room that was used for breaks between meals and prayers. The imam used this space as his own office too, for the just-married couples, for any person who was in trouble and needed help andprayers. It happened that there appeared to be doubtful people who needed more prayers than the others. He would also use it for the little children whenever their mothers complained about them crying too much, the stock when they didn't quite produce milk and so on, and people who were potentail of any evil eyes.

Moreover, he prayed and sang for the dead people. The number of clients became higher and higher with the passing of time. They came from different countries, because he had become famous up to Instanbul. There were also clients from other nationalities that obeyed to the way of healing this imam used. For all those who had problems, he would release them with the word of God.

This room was used as a welcoming inn for any newcomer that needed shelter, to rest and pray, as well. In the middle of the garden there was a deep well, about 12 meters for the ablution before the prayer time. Further down he had built another small facility that surrounded the area in woods so that animals or careless little children didn't come in.

At the same place, next to this, in the northern part there was the Vakëf land of three acresthe same surrounded and reserved for a future cemetery.

The grass was mown twice within a year. With the money earned from the grass sold, the mosque was well-maintained. There was an open barn where some reserve food was kept for the necessities of people going by with carriages and animals, bulls and horses. They would stop there and feed the stock. In the Mejtep of this mosque he prepared the next generation of the imams from other villages of the area. Everyone coming there had a bit of experience but needed work to be done so, he would teach and prepare them to sit the exam and with their knowledge to take the diploma for becoming an imam.

In a way, he cooperated with the Madrasah "Isa Begu" of Skopje. His students were mainly of a considerable age or had good experience in any of the mosques of the time. Given the test from this well known imam they would gain the right to study and to get a degree as an imam from the board commission of the teachers of this Madrasah.

The education of new imams led to the creation of new possibilities of the opening of new mosques in other villages and to serve at least two people there.

One was the Imam and the other was Muezzin. Seeing that new mosques were being opened and new villages were developing with his contribution made him feel proud and happy. The father of Ymer had graduated in the Madrasah "Isa Begu", and was declared Honoured

Teacher and outside Collaborator of this Medrese. Thus, Ymer took his first lessons at the same school, as his father and his grandfather.

Ymer was the last one in the family who preached in the Arabic language and alphabet. He boasted for the fact that he had preserved with fanaticism the traditons of the predecessors of the patriarchal families and the last one to preach Islam generation after generation with the same HolyBooks inherited by his grandfather and father. He noticed that new generations were rising in higher levels. They gained knowledge beyond religion such as arts, history, biology, physics, biology, mathematics, geography, astronomy and other fields, translating the HolyWritings in their native language.

Very often he would face resistence from the youngsters who were studying these writings and tried to stop them because he noticed that the religious aspect in the village was having troubles. Thus, he would speak to people, personally or in mejteps that the only knowledge that is acceptable for God derives from the Glorious Quran and that any other form of information is unacceptable, because it comes from atheists and seculars. He struggled to defend the idea that Islam should be preached and be written only in Arabic letters because it is the most preferred language to God and Prophet Muhamedi Alejselam was sent by Allah and spoke this blessed language.

The circumstances had changed now and time was different. He started to preach in his own language and to write in Albanian. Except for coments and parts of the Holy Book many fake writings were discovered, so they weren't translated. He protested in a silent way, but powerless to the crowds that were in exhaliation.

With the formation of the Islamic Communities and the education of the new generations in the native language new schools and Madrasahwere opened in the Albanian language. The interested ones abandoned private lessons they used to take from the peachers. In Pristina, the first High School "Alaudin" was opened, providing full time lessons in Albanian and in a few years of time the first imams started giving their own lessons.

They preached in the native language and a few years later they started working in the field. They taught the verses, the parts of Quran, they made forums, workshops, and seminars and so on. Thinking that the oriental way of preaching was changing these preachers had to accept the new changes and conditions of time.

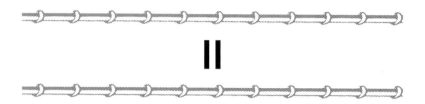

II

One day Ymer's sister got married in Preseva. According to the tradition, people came to her house for greetings. He stayed there for two weeks. He noticed that each night one of his nephews studied the History of Pristina, he learned until late at night. Curious, he once approached to his son. He noticed that he was reading something in the Latin alphabet, the one which Ymer couldn't understand. He thought that certain such books opposed Islam.

"My dear son, why do you tire yourself reading such books of Latin letters that are against our religion? These books oppose the religious principles. It's a shame that you, the nephew of an imam read books opposing the Muslim religion."

-Uncle, these books do not have offensive character but national one."

Being aware that he was in exams' term he said to Ymer: -Dear uncle, in three weeks I have to sit an exam so I am preparing for it. Please do not interrupt or impede me.

The uncle answered: -What do you learn in those useless books that have nothing to do with the Glorious Quran?

-No, uncle, here I learn real things that have happened throughout history. I learn about the history of Albania here, about heroes and wise people in our entire history.

-Yes, yes, I know, you learn about those who worked and fought against Turkey. -the uncle said.

-No, no they fought for their country.

-So who are they? -the uncle asked.

-My uncle, you know these heroes quite well. For sure at that time you were a child so you must have heard about them fighting against the occupators who wanted to take our lands andevict us. All slavic elaborates are well known, be them individuals or groups of legal formations supported and financed by Russians, Serbians and the Turkish government who did everything to reach their barbarian scopes for the eviction of the Albanian population beyond Anadoll. So, the enemy has worked hard in order to denationalize us from our lands.

-Ok, but who is the enemy?-the uncle asked. Please tell me. All these books are written by your enemies?You believe these books don't you? Do not believe these books my dear son, -Ymer said.

We have to leave this country- he continued-we have to go in Sacred Places countries, where the Arabic language is spoken, and the language of God. The boy raised his eyes and looked at Ymer angrily. "Sorry uncle, but that's not the truth! I don't agree with you! These are propaganda of the enemies; Turkish and Macedonian people in cooperation with all these other enemies. I consult with these books, with the heroes and well known men of the country.

-Don't tell me these, because it's religion what gives you light and sends you near God! Who are they, tell me?

-They are all from Albanian lands, but there are from our parts too. - The nephew said and started counting them with his fingers. These are: Idriz Seferi, Mulla Idrizi, Isa Boletini, Hasan Prishtina, Mulla Fetahu, Vesel Bajraktari, XheladinKorbalia, Ibrahim kelmendi, Sulë Hotla, Shaip Mustafa, Selami Hallaçi, Jet Rainca, Dan Samolica, Avdulla Presheva etc. Do not forget that I study this Albanian history secretly, illegally because we are forbidden, so I study it in Pristina. Ymer stepped back looking at his son in distance and was surprised how he knew all those names of famous people that were forbidden to be mentioned in public. He took off the hat and took out a handkerchief from the inner pocket.

-Can you read me something more about these people because you know your uncle can't read in Albanian Alphabet?

-Of course, -the nephew answered. -Listen uncle I will explain you what I have read because I don't have this book at home. Mulla Idriz Gjilani through religious education gathered all Albanians without religion differentiation and fought till death for the joining of the Albanian lands. Ymer was all ears. He was contradicting his image as an imam and fought till death for the unity of the Albanian territories. -Continue continue- (he said to his nephew.

-He was a very decisive person, very knowledgeable to write and a real fighter in his ideals especially for the mountains of Karadak which he defended with words, weapons and blood. He was invincible. The nephew raised his voice speaking in order to attract his uncle and convince him that he was talking about a very strong man. He continued talking about Mulla Idriz Gjilanin who never surrendered in front of enemies. He told him how he became a legend as a political spiritual and military leader. He found a brochure where the biography of Mulla Idrizi, which he read loud and with clear voice. He didn't raise his head until he finished it as a whole. When finished, he saw tears in his uncle's face. He apologised. The uncle got more emotional and hugged his son and started laughing and got more emotional.

-Do you know why I am crying my son? Because of Mulla Idriz heroism and all the words you read. This made feel proud. If only I had studied at school like you have done!! I have never known that my nephew is so well-educated.

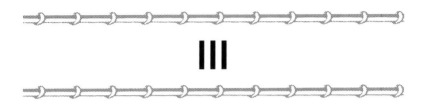

III

His goal was that his son, Dema, after having finished the elementary school successfully, was interested to enroll him to the MadrasahHigh School "Alaudin" in Prishtina. He wasn't calm and he continuously thought about sending his son to the capital, to motivate him to be a devoted educator of the Islamic religion, and even a patriot like Mulla Idriz Gjilani. He worried more and more everyday because he had information that it was too difficult to be registrated in this school which was the only of this kind in Kosovo.

The competition was significantly difficult and only three three candidates would be accepted from each Municipality. Late at night he couldn't sleep and during the day he also thought ofpossible solutions. He had been discussing about this problem with other imam colleague from the suburbs, because the person who promised to help him had passed away.

What gave him hope was that he discussed with a lot of people who had promised him to help in this direction. He missed a lot of family traditions for imams and his desire was to realize the last will of his father and his grandfather so he couldn't get peace, because his last will was one of the most compulsory obligations which the HolyBooks say and under any conditions should be realized until its implementation.

One day good news came from one of his friends, an imam too, who had some friends that they had relations to this medrese. They had found a way to accept his son part time, because there was no free place for regular lessons.

This gave him courage again because his son would be registered and would finish this school and would gain the title Imam of the Mosque. He took the right address and set the day when to leave for it.

Firstly, he thought to leave alone and find the proper living place for his son, but in the last moment he changed mind and decided to take his son with him. He chose to do so because he wanted to present him in front of the MadrasahBoard and convince them that his son had the elementary degreeand some knowledge in reading-writing in Arabic language. He knew the mainDuá. He knew how to pray and lots of other things that have to do with Islam, because such knowledge it was him, whohad taught to his son regarding the Elementary Islamic Religion Lessons. The next day in the morning, after prayer time, he left for the capital together with his son.

The journey was long;it took two hours by bus. Dema was surprised at the bus journey. It was the first time in his life leaving the house and traveling so long by bus. He was so curious about the things he could view during the journey by the bus windows and experienced special emotions. He was eager to see how a big city looked like. Ymer had fallen asleep because he hadn't slept well for days. He slept until the end of the journey when the conductor told them that they already arrived to Prishtina. He pulled a paper out of his pocket where he had the address written in Arabic language and started to ask the first local about the Medrese. The persondirected him to the Mosque which was approximately 200 meters further and said:

-Go there because they know where the Madrasahis.

In the mosque they met the imam, who presented himself:

-I am Mulla Cani, an imam of this Mosque. Welcome! Thanks to Allah that brought you here in this moment. A kind reception, while they told him about their problem.

-Don't worry, we will go there together. I have people who work for us, -said the Imamtapping Dema's on the shoulders. Happy you for this precious boy!

Ymer was surprised by the warm welcome and the optimistic words of the Imam Cani which gave him an optimistic spark.

After having lunch, the Imam sent Ymer together with his son to the Madrasah. There he met the Council and the Board of the HighSchoolMadrasah"Alaudin", who welcomed them respectfully. After the introduction and greetings, Ymer said:

-I am Dema's nephew, one of the well known Imams of our Nahije, while my only son got his name. It is the last will from the deceased Dema that father and grandfather to have Imams in the family and the tribe. This was transmitted to me also asthe last will, so I haveinherited this obligation and theImam's name. That's why I brought him and in the name of the God, I ask you to accept him if this is possible.

The board's headmaster was taught with these words as a refrain because each parent who brought their children for the first time to enroll in this religious school. Withoutfinishingthe thought, Ymeraddedquickly:

-For sure we will accept the grand-nephew of the person who sacrificed himself for Islam and the delivery of Islam on these parts. Ymer's heart joyed from this welcome with these good words about his grandfather and he filled with pride. After being assured, he was released from allcomplexities he had had until those moments. They remembered him that there were no free places for regular pupils, but only part time and meanwhile he would try to take regular lessons.

Ymer didn't understand the word part time and asked for clarification.

He said: "Well–to begin first then, - did something with hand as he was pushing something inside.

Ymer kindly accepted the conditionsbowing his head. Now his main trouble was to accommodate his son into a bedroom the nearest to the school possible. Before he left from the round table he asked to be directed to any Inn for some days until he found a room to rent for his son. The Board of the school offered Ymer a free bedroom which was reserved for the pupils to sleep that night.

They gladly accepted the offer and the service of the SchoolBoard. At night, Ymer didn't sleep because he was still worried of how to find a bedroom for his son.

The next day, Mulla Cani appeared again. After he greeted friendly using the Arabic phrase, he told the purpose of coming and invited them to go to his Mosque. As they satcomfortable neara fountain under the shadow of a big lime, he said to Ymer:

-I have a proposal for your son to live in the facilities of this Mosque.

- Look there-, he pointed with his hand to the building, here we have a bedroom, a small kitchen, a bathroom and all the basicsupplies to live in, because they are all inside of this small facility and it's all what a small family needs for living.The most importantis that everything is free and he has nothing to pay for. Food is provided as well bythecongregation!

This offer was unbelievable to Ymer. He was all eyes and ears…. "The most precious thing is that I" -he raised his hand and touched himself and with the other hand he touched Dema's head and brought him close to himself then said:

-I will teach him to practice the work of a Muezzin, because Ihavealready got the basic preparation for this child. I will take care for your son like he was mine. Don't worry because we will make him an excellent and devoted Imam. But to make this happen he has to follow my advice and that of other counsellors of this Mosque! We will help him until he can be enough prepared by himself as according to the Glorious God we are obliged to help each-other. Based on the offer made by Imam Cani, Ymer was so happy andso proud of this great chance that was offered to his son. Drops of happiness' tears fell from his eyes, and quite spontaneously he stood up and hugged Mulla Cani and personally thanked him and gave him the blessing that only God would reward him for this humanitarian and helpfuldecision.

After he made an inspection to the building in which his son would live, Ymer was fascinated from what he saw. He just entered inside the narrow hallway to the right, opened the main door and a spacious room appeared with a hige window covered with green silk curtains. The biggest part of the floor was covered by a handmade carpet of light green colour which was handmade, and in the end of the room near the wall there was this large mattress covered by a green blanket too and a small bedside cabinet next to the bed with a lamp upon it, while at the other corner there was some large furniture with Arabic inscriptions written. Ymer took one of the books, the biggest one and saw it emotionally, then sat down and started to speak something in Arabic language and kissed it three times repeating the same words and carefully returned it to the previous place without hurting it. While in front of the main entrance there was a narrow door and the biggest part of it was of glass. Inside there was a normal bathroom paved with green tiles and in sequence: bathtubs, WC and the porcelain sink. On the top part almost in ceiling there was a green small window which touched the ceiling. On the left there was a big room in a salon form with a big table and eight chairs rounded by leather armchairs. Further, with a removable wall in a harmonious form, inside there was the kitchen in which there were: the stove/cooker, the fridge and a small table with wooden old chairs.

Ymer was flying from joy when he thought that all these were for his son. He didn't have these objects in his home in the village. Finally he was disposed. The time to turn back home came. He asked for the approval to leave convinced that he is leaving his son in safe hands, thanking Mulla Cani for his humanitarian and material gesture. Even Mulla Cani accepted gladly Ymer's gratitude.

-Now you have to leave, Dema and I will get to the bus station.

During the way to the bus station, the young Dema was surprised by the magnificence of the city. He for the first time had a contact with a big living place like this one, full of people in the streets, with high buildings and wide and fair roads, with cars and lights everywhere. Everything went fast. People walked into different directions and no one was stumbled. Everyone went to his own work. He was surprised by everything he could see wondering how many people the city had. Ymer left with nostalgia being separated from his son and Mulla Cani with pride, because he left his son in the safe hands. After he entered the bus, he turned back again like he has forgotten something. He once again addressed to the son with nostalgia:

-Listen my son, I am leaving you in the hands of the God, of theImam and of the people who promised to support you, but please, do not surrender yoursef to everyday pleasures such as parties and the careless and rampant life of this big city!

I really want you to be like my grandfather whose name you have inherited. Do not mortify his name and us. As a family we desire that you go to school and succeed honouring us amd the entire country as well."

He went on apologizing to the attendees. Dema spoke nothingbut just listened with bowed headin front of his father. Apparently heput those words in any drawer of his memory. He had nostalgia because he was leaving home for the first time without greeting to his mother, sisters and friends who he played with every day.

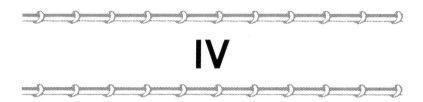

IV

Days passed by and Dema was well taught and respected by the people. Not only did he accept their terms and conditions but he fulfilled his duties very dedicated as well. Very precise and devoted in his religious mission, he was the first who opened the door of the mosque early in the morning, jumped in to the minaree and asked for the Morning Prayer. He cleaned the Mosque every day after the MorningPrayer. Not hesitating he called all the meals, starting with breakfast, lunch, and dinner in the end. This was the way he invited people to come to the meals pray. He was the first to open and the last to close that door. Then he went to his room. There he read and got prepared to keep lectures from any part of the Glorious Quran. He spent most of his time in the Mosque. He cleaned and kept the sworn order very well which he had put himself as an obligation. He became the central figure after congregation and everyone honored and respected him....Even though he was too young, only a 16-year-old boy, he was brave and very effwctive in communication. He looked like his father and gained the hearts of all who came to pray in the Mosque. The number of people participating incongregation was on the growth. A lot of things changed in his life. Now he forgot the life he used to live in his hometown. In his village, the number ofcongregationwas quite reduced. Here it was different. The Mosque was bigger and each day full of congregation, while on Fridays there were no free places for all people so they used the oudoor areas to pray too. Dema's skills were used by Mulla Cani as well, because Dema was a correct and hardworking student.

The congregation respected him a lot! Every day food was brought from volunteers. After the earlyMorning Prayers they often invited him at their houses for dinner. So, good friendship was established between Dema and the congregation. Usinghis melancholic voice attracted believers more and more. Because of thepure and beautiful melody of his voice, they started to invite him to sing mevlude. After the ceremony he earned some money. But the best part was that people were grateful. This motivated him to adore the initial profession more. For this, he received a reminder from the Imam, who clearly told him:-You can't take gratitude given in the name of theMosqueaway from my presence. I will receive all benefits and we will share them together. Dema acknowledged the Imam's advice and regretted.

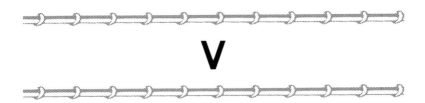

V

A few months after serving in the Mosque, theBoard offers him the position of the muezzin, appointing him a low-key salary. Now Dema was given greater responsibilities under the same terms and conditions and rules offered and appointed by his uncle. Apart from the working days he worked during the whole week, and he had a day of the week off. He gained experience everyday and thus he became a responsible adult. He was in contact with older people so he gained knowledge and advice from them.

One day, a devoted old man who came there regularly and prayed for the five times of day, teased Dema as he was cleaning the floor. He said:

-Young boy, you need someone here to help you! You can not live like this, you need someone to take care of you. We need to find a good girl for you so that she helps you with everything. A devoted Muslim should create his family when the right time comes.

Dema smiled and approved his words.

One evening the old man said to Dema that we were going to visit him for dinner but that this should be a secret. This made Dema think. He was curious about what the old man was thinking and planning. Why nobody should know about this dinner?! The next day after the prayer, the old man was the only one left there and he called Dema saying:

-Shall we go! Are you ready!

-Yes! –Dema replied.

This was the second time Dema visited the house of the old man, but this time it was different. As soon as they got in, there was a very nice smell of very different dishes inside the house. All the family was there apart from the old man's son who lived abroad in Germany and only came once a year to visit his father and family. The niece of the old man was serving the food. Everytime her eyes met those of Dema she had a reddish expression in her face. Dema looked at her time and again and her beauty made him feel different. Her golden hair, half-covered in a yellow napkin went down to her spine. That hair was provoking Dema some very beautiful feelings. Dema didn't eat too much. Apparently he fell in love with the beautiful girl. After finishing dinner Dema prayed and thanked them for everything. Everyone got out of the table and sat in the sofas.

The girl appeared with a big bowl of water and offered to everyone to wash their hands after dinner. When it was Dema's turn she was so confused that the bowl fell from her hands and water spread first on Dema's knees then all over the floor. In trouble she apologized and immediately left the room faking that she was ashamed for what she did.

At the Prayer Time, Dema politely asks to leave and go to the mosque. The very next day the old man tells Dema about the intention he had when he invited him for dinner.

-I would like to match you with my niece, - he said. Dema's face became reddish and didn't know what to say.

-I would like to discuss it with my family first then I can give you an answer.

Once a month Dema went to the village to see his family. Any time he went there it was a day of joy, happiness and pride for his family.

But this time was a bit different. He went to see the family with a completely dfferent mission and happier than other days. His mother, noticed an unusual sparkling shine in his eyes, she hugged and kissed him and sad proudly:

-Masha-Allah, you have become a real man, ready for marriage. We should find a girl for marriage as soon as we can!

These words made it easier for Dema so he immediately told his mother about the offer of the old man. He told her he had already seen the possible future wife and that she was a beautiful young lady. The mother once more hugged him and wished him happiness.

He stayed at home for only two nights then he left to the capital to continue with his mission but this time more energetic. He now was illusioned about the beautiful girl. He knew the mother's reaction and the fact that she was quite happy about the news he had given.

Meanwhile the old man talked to the Imam as well, telling him his idea of marriage between Dema and his niece. But, the Imam was shocked o what he heard and he disagreed in a convinced way.

-What made you think of ths? Who ased you to find a girl for Dema? I ave taught and prepared Dema to have him like a real son, to become an Imam, not to become your son-in-law. Do you understand? And please don't mock with me again. –he said disappointed. –In short I have promised to give him my daughter. –Mulla Cani finished.

The old man stepped back feeling guilty as he wasn't aware of the situation.

-Forget about this and do tell nobody!

These were the last words of the Imam to the old man who left disappointed and unhappy.

As soon as Dema arrived, he told the old man about the conversation he had with his family and that they all agreed on the idea being the fac that Dema found he girl ver beautiful. But, to his surprise, he old man discussed with him very openly about what the Imam had said about his own daughter. He said that they should agree on the idea of the Imam as his words couldn't be opposed. Moreover, he was like a real father to Dema. So, he advised Dema to obey the wordsof the Imam.

In this situation, Dema couldn't refuse the offer of Imam, though his heart beat for the niece of the old man.

He got married to the daughter of Imam who once more reminded him the condition that he should serve as a Muezzin in the same mosque, until Imam retired, what needed two more months to happen.

After the narriage took place, someone who looked up to Dema, offered him a land of a small surface, in the neighbourhood of Capi. It was small but enough to build a cottage where he could stay until he made some money for the future. The cottage was constructed withtwo small bedrooms, a house with no windows, neither roar, nor sides. The space wasn't appropriate as there were other houses on both sides. It had only one big glass surface, wall-sized at the front.

It was sorrounded by other houses standing high in front of it, seemingly they could impede even sunrays to enter the house. It needed some lighting and air. It was continuously humid because of the conditions. At the entrance, on the left there was a toilet, built and installed directly over the canalization of waste waters, hence it smelled awful. It was something usual for the people living in such house to smell that. These people were Dema and his wife and the two parents. In rainy days they would get in troubles because water entered inside home from the street and roof, into the ceiling and down inside the room. This also happened to other house as they were next to each other untik the end of the street, part of Capi neighbourhood. Moreiver, very often the cats chased mice from roof to roof running and jumping over them.

Dema got narried to his wife without a wedding ceremeony. It was just the Imam who prayed a Duá wishin his daughter and his son-in-law a happy life.

Though in such difficult conditions, their life continued to flow quiet and happy. Sadia was a good cook and contented with the way Dema treated her. He was happy with her behavoiur as well. He went to work and couldn't wait to get back home just to be with his wife. He knew she would be waiting with the towel ready for him, and she would prepare the table for dinner and this would make them feel comfortable and happy with each other. Years went by in harmony, but there was a problem, the only one in all these years, the fact those nine years since marriage and they didn't have a baby. In this small cottage the cry of a baby missed. However the parents didn't intervene in their relationship though their biggest desire was having grandchildren. Dema's parents spent most if their time with him as Ymer was old enough to be a pensioneer. He was happy with the job his som did in the Capital as a devoted Imam. Very often he would say to his son: -For the moment, here, this is enough for us to leave alone, but when our grandchildren come, should we take them to the village with us or should we find a new bigger house. Years went by and they became hopeless because they still didn't have children, despite all the attempts. They had consulted preachers and traditional doctors. His parents had now lost all their hopes of becoming grandparents one day. Someone had advised them to go and see a gynaecologistbut this was impossible because their religion and tradition didn't allow medicine to interfere in such situation. They could deal with this only devoting to God. Divorce wasn't under any legal basis so it was thought that the best would be to spread the word that this couple was separating due to the inability of the woman to have children, though nine years had passed. At this time everything started to go badand their relation started to be in trouble. Facts were invented very easily, not taking intk consideration the spiritual and psychological cpnsequrnces that these two people would face.

It was said that the wife left home, mugging it and some money, so she was said to be a thief. This would be accepted by her family, an Imam's fanily. To make things appear real they also faked a trick though they weren't so intelligent to do it perfect. The night, when the supposed money was stolen, Fati a cousin living and studying in the Dormitory of Students, was there. He stayed there for the whole weekend because it rained heavily so he was obliged to stay there. On purpose, they insisted Fati stayed for that night so that he was part of the plan as well. Two days later Sadije was accused for stealing the money. The poor woman, thinking that maybe they don't remember where they had left the money searched everywhere but it was useless.

She swore for the sky that she didn't take that money. She was quite tense in front of such accusation.She almost lost her mind. She asked to go to her father's house for a few days to calm down. Sucj wat she would also meet her parents and tell them what had happened. Before leaving she went to the room where her mother-in-law was, and took all her clothes in front of her to convince her that she was leaving taking nothing with her. She asked the mother-in-law to speak with her husband and son about this, to let then know that when she left she had nothing taken with her. The mother-in-law didn't pay too much attention. She wasn't part of the trap so she asked Sadije not to worry as somewhere the moeny would be found and everything would be okay.

-Don't put your family into trouble.-she advised.

Seeing Dema off to the mosque for the Prayer Time, she also accompanied Sadije to the house of her parents. All along the way they had spoken nothing. It was night, silence, and Dema didn'twant other people to listen to them. He refused any of her attempts to explain and convince him that she hadn't stolen the money. Arriving at her parents' house they were surprised to see her coming home so late at night. They asked what had happened and she burst into tears. She sobbed and told them the reason she was there and everything had happened.

-I surrender to you and God only! She asks for support pretending she was innocent. Her father immediately took her hand and together they went to Dema's house for explanations, though it was too late almost midnight. He asked:

-Is there anyone else auspicious?

-No, it's only that last night, a cousin of ours was here. He comes to visit us very rarely. He is a student and being the fact that it was raining heavily we welcomed and asked him to pass the night here as it was impossible to leave at that rainy time. But, the truth is that, for no moment did he leave the room, and moreover he couldn't have known where the money was hidden so it is impossible that he might have taken it.

-Huh, now I understand who is after this, - Mulla Cani said convincingly.

With his initiative, very stubborn he asked for the cousin to be present and to say his words related to this issue. He was one hundred percent sure that he was the one who had taken the money. Sadija was so worried she was about to get into depressiob. She cried and weeped unstoppably. They passed the whole night waiting for Fati's answer. Mulla Cani still insisted:

-I want that person to be here and tell us the truth. It was impossible for Dema to go and take Fati from the Students' Dormitory at that specific time. It was very early in the morning. Three o'clock a.m. He promised the Imam, that as soon as he finished the Morning Prayer he would go to see Fati and bring him home. After sleeping a little, Demagoes to the mosque, prays, then he goes to Fati. It was a day off, because all students were in exams' time. All Fati did was eating and learning. He didn't get out of the dormitory. Very often he went to the bookstore to read.

At the time Dema arrived he found Fati sleeping together with his two friends in the same room. He invited Fati to his house as his father wanted to ask about something. Fati, still asleep, asked to know what it was about:

-What has happened? Is there anything to worry?

-No, no -Dema repiled.

-But, what does he want to ask me about? For sure something has happened but you don't want to tell me about it.

-Don't worry, nothing has happened. Come with me, we'll go somewhere to do something.

He got dressed silently, not to awake his friends, and started together with Dema to the Capi Neighbourhood which was approximately four kilometers far from Dema's house. Dema was six years older than Fati, the latter respected him. Leaving, Fati once more asked:

-Are you sure there is nothing to worrt?

-Yes, yes, -Dema replied.

-Then how come you appeared so early in the morning?- Fati asked.

-I was at the mosque, I prayed and to save time I came now.

-But what does he want from me. I was there only last night.

-I know nothing either, - Dema said.

-Ok then.

Now Fati was calm and kept walking contented that at least nothing bad had occurred. He thought that most likely he had been called to go to Dema's house for any order that the family had for his own family when he went to the village. This neighbourhood was in the north-western part of the city. The turning point that led to Dema's house was a narrow street where you could only walk on foot. It was covered in gravel by the inhabitants of the area. There was mud everywhere sticking in the shoes, and poodles of waste waters. All the street smelled awfully. Alost ten meter far from home, Dema appeared in front of Fati and spoke:

-Do you wan to know the truth of your arrival here?

-Sure. I asked you about it and you told me you knew nothing… Tell me.

Dema revealed:

-Last night aconsiderable amount of money has been stolen. Being the fact that you slept in our house, we are doubtful whether it was you or Sadija who took them.

Hearing these words Fati lost all positive feelings. It seemed to him as if someone was tricking him. Hence, it was about a problem. He got scared. His heart beat fast like that of a bird. What was this?! Was it a trap?!

He turned to Dema all in a different tone, a tone of hate and hostility:

-Why didn't you tell me when I asked, but just now in front of your house?

He found all this so little serious, he couldn't believe Dema's words so he asked again:

-Are you telling the truth or are you just provoking me?!

-I am serious, but I don't even klnow, why didn't I tell you,-he answered confused.

-What do you want from me? Why should I get ionside if you consider me a thief. I don't think I can keep to this accusation. Ok, I'll go in. But, how can I go inside. What for? This was so unexpected. What should I do?

He felt his feet heavy. Entering the house he heard Sadije sobbing. It was like someone crying for a deceased. It was complete silence except for Sadije who kept crying and weeping, sitting on her knees there at the corner of the room, with fuzzy hair, hitting the pavement klike she was gone mad. That room seemed so small to Fati now, almost suffocating. This space wasn't enough for all these people.

Sadije's father was sitting on the front, pale and worried. He stood cross legged and on the other side of the wall, on the right there was Dema's father. Time and again he scratched his head as if there was something there to tease him. He seemed as he was tempting to remove something, whereas the father of Sadije looked quite tense and nervous. He looked like he was waiting something impatiently. These two men were both Imams and they both served the two greatest mosques of the capital. They stood silent. It was only Sadije who at times broke the silence groaning profoundly. They had nothing to say, words had finished. As soon as Fati entered the room, she immediately went out in the dark hall, as if she was escaping from him, and starts tidying up all the shoes that were outside the room. Fati neared to greet. He approached to shake hands with the people that were there but they behaved rudely and none of them shook hands with Fati. They ingored him instead. In this condition, he went to sit on the other side of the wall, opposite to Dema's father. Dema himself sat just at the entrance and just like a policeman bringing the accused in front of the judges spoke:

-Here I brought the man you wanted.

Surprised Fati aske:

-What is happening here? How can I help you? What do you want from me sirs?

All these questions were interrupted by Sadije entering with a pale and desperate face, win which all signs of deep worry were clearly seen. She had been crying all night. Her beauty of only two nights ago was faded in just one night and she was now in a bad psychological situation. Fati felt pity for her and he just wanted to scream:

-What did you do to this woman, May God punish you!!!

But thoughts were interrupted when his eyes met hers. So many tears had she cried that night, she looked like a shadow now. There was noone she could complain. The father couldn't believe her words, though several times she had announced her mother that she noticed something was being arranged in order to force her leave the house. However, her mother replied, reminding her that she was the girl and the daughter-in-law of Imams, and the wife of a Muezzin, so it wasn't appropriate for her to have such pretentions.

-Never say this again, - she said once.

She drew back and finally obeyed to the mother. This time was different. She dared to get in front of her father and said:

-Please father, don't ask me to continue because I am fed up with everything. I am just a victim. Please father does understand me!

She kept sobbing, what made her change the tone of voice as well:

-Things are now over; I can't go on like this. Don't do wrong to me and Fati. He is innocent and I am innocent. Believe me, father.

At some point she stopped, she went out to get some fresh air, and then came back with new ideas. She told them that maybe Fati has been involved in the trap just to make it more believeable and to help them accuse her for the crime.

-I still don't believe it, - she directed to Fati apologising.

She moved around. Inside that small dark room, her curly hair covered with the yellow napkin looked so fuzzy like she had just gone out of the psychiatry room. However, she apporached to Fati and shook hands with him, saying nothing but just sobbing. She steps back hiding her tears. In this situation, her father intwerrupts:

-Why do you shake hands with a bastard thief?!-pointing at Fati, -and you dare asking what has happened?! Aren't you ashamed stealing your cousins and dishonour my daughter?!

Fati's cheeks, front, neck even ears blushed. He raised his head up and murmured as if he had a strong and heavy weight on his back. For the first time in his life, he was being accused for something he hadn't done. He looked at those white heads, those beards, unshaved... he thought: "Are these people aware of the adventure they are undertaking on behalf of doubts and defamation. How can I escape this unexpected situation?!"

He was so under pressure. He finally asked for a glass of water to cool down. Drinking the water he focused his eyes on just one point in the ceiling trying to find salvation there. Everything contradicted the truth. His face looked pale and worried more and more. He stared at these people, well-known as Imams, religious people who are regarded as religious by the majority of simple people who obey and admire them.

"Now I am standing in front of these people accusing me for a crime I haven't comitted. And they do this incapable of proving it with facts.do these people really believe in God? How do they try to convince others about their convinctions putting all their moral power and consciousness?"

He had a sense of injustice that had never felt before. He tried to defend but how could he? They accused him and they accused him much more when he tried to defend himself. He kept questioning himself how could it be possible that Imams were so bad people at a time everyone obeyed, admired and trusted them, took lessons and preaches from them. He knew he was a victim of such scenario. He tightened his fingers, he could hit a rock. Yes, at that very moment he could punch a rock. He gritted his teeth. Images of aplay tragical-comic appeared to him. Now he recovered from the pain, and again asked himself:

-do these people cause pain to others and they don't even know about this?

"Which is the problem right now?"

He didn't really know how to solve the situation so he said to them:

-For the first time I hear such accusation! I haven't stolen any money.

Mulla Cani was absolutely furious. He didn't let him finish the sentence, he hit the floor, from which different insects came out and ran away, and spoke loudly and angrily:

-Take out the money now, otherwise we will call the police!

He thought himself like he was in a dream, where three men, who were supposed to be religious men, serving in the House og God, spreading the word of God, who were always followed and adored by other people, and to whom other people found consolation and soultion for their problems either physical or psychological were accusing him for a crime he knew nothing about.

-I am innocent. I have nothing to do with this. How can I react and where can I complain if such influential people accuse me?! Nobody will believe me and the accusation will be more serious if I complain. – He thought.

The cousin and his son spoke nothing. This convinced Mulla Cani as well. Fati's thoughts were interrupted by the softened voice of the Imam, this time different from the previous. He looked like he was repented and apologised:

-You better bring the money; it's not too late yet.

Fati felt his heart beat fast and said: - I haven't taken the money. Please understand me

-Well,-Imam said.- Are you able to swear on the sacred book the Glorious Quran, that you haven't taken the money?

He kneeled down these ghosts who were oppressing all the good manners and behaviour, morals and principles they had showed during their elite lives.

- What is this nonsense?! I am able to do whatever is needed because I am pure like crystal water.

Sadija stood up convinced that he was innocent and trying to stop her father from the injustice he was doing to the poor boy.

-Don't qaccuse him, he hasn't taken the money. Their only aim is to make me leave the house. This is the truth, -she said with tears in her eyes.

But her father thought different and spoke angrily:

-You stay there, shut up and don't try to defend the thief, othervwise you'll burn in the Xhehenem fire.

She insisted on the truth:

-Father please, let's get out of this house!

He threatened the daughter a second time:

-Shut up!

She stepped back, not complying with the words of her father

-Now, this boy will swear for the truth on the sacred book, the Glorious Quran. You will see the terrible consequences you'll have a few days after, if you fake such oath. Shame on you, shame! I know how school teaches you on stealing and offending the others.

Dema and his father spoke nothing. They acted like casual spectators. They only listened to the judgement of the Imam.

-I will do the oath, -Fati finally spoke.

He decided to do such, thinking and hoping that things would end there, with the oath. He asked what he had to do. The Imam stood up, went to the drawer where he kept some religious books of arabic alphabet, took a thick book covered in plastic, kissed it three times, nearing it to the front in rows, and said something in arabic. He put the book on a small table, the exact size of the book. And he asked:

-Have you ever sworn on a scared book before?

-Never, -Fati replied,- this is the very first time.

-Careful, think about it once more, because in case you fake the oath, you will have the greates of problems in a very near future.

-Do what I say then repeat what I say three times in row.

-Agreed, - Fati said. He asked him to say "Bismilah!" and to put the right hand on the Glorious Quran and to repeat three times in row:

"VALLAHI, BILAHI, TALLAHI. *I have not taken the money!* Fati spoke loud, his voice echoed inside the room's walls.

The Imam intervened asking him not to shout, but Fati said that this was best so that God would hear well his Dua. After finishing the oath, Fati felt released and calmed from the trouble he was a few moments ago. Proud and happy he asked:

-Are you happy now?

Sadije's father said:

-Yes, we'll be happy when, in a very short time, you'll have very serious problems for faking an oath on the Quran.

This answer was irritating, it weighed so much on Fati's shoulders and mind and innocent soul. Finally, he understood that there was no other way to convince those men about the truth. However he gained courage after the oath, so he directed to the three of them:

-I have a request for you all.

They looked surprised at one another.

-Speak!

-Should women swear on this?

It was clear that he thought that Sadije could be the one to blame, though he felt sorry for saying that. Her father interrupted:

-She has no need to swear because I guarantee for her. I assure anyone that my daughter is well-educated and would never do such things.

Sadija insisted:

-No, no, I want to make the oath too.

-Stay there; -her father spoke loud grabbing her attention. She saw Quran on the table and ran to swear. She repeated the same procedure as Fati, weeping. In the end she cursed her husband and father-in-law for this injustice. Fati, with the courage of a strong invincible man asked loud:

-Do you dare to make the oath that you are telling the truth as well. You say you always tell the truth, isn't it?

-Shame on you! -Sadije's father shouted. -How do you dare questioning our word, our truth?! We are religious people, how do you dare?! Nobody has ever tried to question our truths until today. There are hundreds of congregations following us. Whoever you ask about us, will guarantee that we do nothing without facts and proofs. Shame, shame and blame on you!

-I will tell you only one thing, -Fati directed to the three men, he was more furious with Sadije's father. After doing the oath he felt more courageous.

-Remember you committed a crime blaming me for something I have never thought of, neither done. You broke my heart! Such accusation is to me a knife on my back. I will have this bruise for my entire life.

Sadije interrupted:

-Please father, don't blame him any longer, I am so sure about his innocence, as I am for mine. These people no longe want me here that is why they made up the whole story. The only reason is our ten-year-old marriage and the fact that we couldn't have children along. They want to kick me out of home. Let's get out of this house immediately. I will assure about the trth and I can swear on that wherever you ask me to.

She stood up crying. Fati spoke nothing. He stood up as well and left the room silent. However, deep inside, his heart was burning. Absolutely tired, emotionally and physically he left to go to his place, to the city center, at the the students' dormitory. He was extremely worried and desperate. Being in such condition, on his way back, he stood somewhere, calmed down for a few minutes and then continued to walk. After, he stood up, found the strength to walk tall and staright, proud of him, though he had just been accused. He knew he was innocent. He felt a voice speaking to him, giving him courage and good faith that the truth would come out one day. Though the streets were full of people, he felt like he was the one, the hero walking towards justice. As soon as he arrived at the building he considered himself a winner. All his friends noticed something was wrong as he entered the dormitory. One of them asked if there was something to worry but he answered quite calm:

-No, nothing has happened.

Though it was late evening, it was dark earlier than usually. The three friends were now preparing to go to the students' restaurant to have dinner. They asked Fati to join them. He reasoned that he wasn't hungry and that he needed to rest a bit, so he didn't join them. Staying alone in the room, he started talking to the accusators:

-How do you dare accusing me of something I haven't done?! Where should I complain for people to understand that this isn't true?! – he walked up and down the room, with a furious face.

Tired, he lied in his bed. He was lost in thoughts, but apparently sleep embraced his body very quickly. He still couldn't stop thinking of what was blowing his mind. He dreamt of the three men accusing him. They sent him to the police station. He reacted: - No, please, I haven't taken them.

He woke up. His friend came close to calm him, gave him a glass of water then finally he gained consciousness. One of the friends, a student of the Medicine School neared to him trying to console and learn what was going on.

-Did you get any bad news or what? -He asked.

Fati asked to be left alone, letting them know there was something that he just couldn't say tell them. During the night he still had some probles with the sleep. The days onward he started to stay alone, apart from his friends. He didn't even read as much as before. He didn't go out with friends and he gave no signs of optimism. For three days he didn't get out of his dormitory room. He liked being alone, and spoke to himself getting no response of course. He became too pessimistic, to the extent that he even thought of interrupting the studies. This situation was distinguished by one of his professors, who once advised him to see a psychologist. At first Fati didn't want to, but later with some persistence he accepted.

He went to see the psychologist, and two consultatiosn he started to feel better, the first signs of improvement were obvious. The doctor advised him to interrupt the studies for a few weeks so he goes back to his village, feels and enjoys nature. He said nothing to his faily and relatives because he knew if he did that would worsen the situation. Instead, his doctor advised him to talk about his proble with other elderly people, though unknown, they could help hi giving advice based on the experience that these people have during their lifetime. He did that, conversed with wise men who were able to suggest and advise him about the best, and to make him feel better, releasing his spiritual pain.

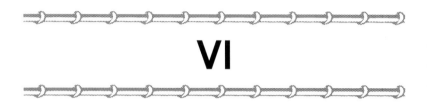

VI

Sadije also protested to the accusation made to her as sson as she left her husband's home. She convinced her father about the truth:

-Fati and I are not responsible of this, I a sure and I can swear on the Sacred Book that this is just a trap to make leave home. There is no place left for me in this house.

The father convinced but on one condition:

-Within a week they would hear about the consequences of the fake oath Fati had done.

They left the house. A week later Imam Cani knocked on their door again to get information about Fati's ongoing, but knew nothing.

Leaving the house he cursed the whole family and apologized to his daughter. He regretted all the accusations he had done to Fati, and asked God for forgiveness.

Thus the long-term friendship and kinshiphe had with Dema and his family was ruined. Dema sold his house and together with his parents moved to another city, where he was appointed Imam. There, he got arried again and had two twins. This was a great surprise to all the family. A few years later other children were born, so the faily grew bigger and happier.

The relationship between Dema and Fati remained broken forever. Fati also got married and created his family. He lived in the same city as Dema but further. At this stage of life Ymer passed away happy for the realized wish leaving behind many grandchildren. Dema was quite active and became on ombudsman. He also became a professor at the University of Orientalistic. But one day he got caught by the Serbian bands and was never found. The family tried to find him but never did.

One day Fati goes to the Children Hospital with his wife and daughter for a check up. There he meets a woman with a two or three-year-old children. The children played together. Fati's daughter was playing with a doll, whereas the other girl starts crying for that doll, so Fati goes close giving the child his daughter's toy in order to calm her cries. The woman, wearing a long dress and a head-scarf, so her face was easily distinguished, approached to Fati and speaks:

-How are you Fati?

-Fine, fine,-he says, confused, hearing his name from a woman he doesn't know.

-And this woman with this little girl, who are they?

-My wife,-Fati answers still confused.

-So, you got married, and you even have a baby?

-Sorry, may I ask who you are?

-Don't you recognize me?- she says,- it's me, Sadije. Don't you remember me?

Her pale face and deep eyes filled with tears. Fati was surprised.

-Oh, yes, now I recall you! I' sorry for not recognizing you!

-This is my mother,- she said, turning to her mother and informing her about Fati and his family. Her mother had been a friend of his other as well, so she asked him about her but he answered:

-My beloved mother passed away several years ago.

She was sorry; she started appraising Fati's mother for being an excellent woman. She thought about an Albanian expression saying that if it is eant to be people meet despite circumstances. Sadije accepted the doll as a gift for her daughter and said:

-I've got three children now, two boys and a girl. I live a happy life, though in poverty. She confessed that her father had passed away two years before and she apologized for the accusation once her father had done towards him. Late had he understood the truth! Quite often he would pray to God for forgiveness for this sin because he considered it a sin having blamed someone for a crime not committed.

With such words, full of pain and emotions they said goodbye to each other. She apologized in the name of her father. She was now happy. Fati, full of emotions expressed all goods wishes for her life and said he was happy that at least her father had understood and accepted the truth. But in the end he said:

-I hope God has forgiven your father, because the pain it left to me has become part of my boold and flesh.

THIRD PART

Sami

It was the second week of January 1998.

The whole country had been under extremely low temperatures for three days. Freezing, icy, everything seemed white as snow. Stalagmites looked like long candles from roofs to ground. Any cat meowing would echo together with the wind. Walls and roofs rubbed from the wind. That wind, that strong wind together with everything sorrounding would create solemn beautiful music like the Fifth Symphony of Beethoven flowing with the snow flakes.

The fumes of chimneys flew before reaching the air. After the cold there was only white snow in the streets which was dangerous forpeople, who those days would only get out of their homes only for a very neccessary reason. Everyone stayed home during all the harsh freezing winter. Fati was home alone. His wife had gone to her family. It was the end of the first half of year. He was lying in the sofa watching the news on TVP (National Televison of Pristina) which announced that the snow was heavy and roads blocked everywhere, and it wasn't advisable to go out in the cold.

Suddenly, he heard the cough of a woman, not very clear because of the wind. He went to the window and saw Lena, the wife of his neighbour. She often came to his house for water when she didn't have at hers. She was wearing a pretty old pair of shoes torn at the top, you could see the fingers covered in woolen socks, like *Luli i vocerr*. She was walking slowly, leaning on the right and on the left with her plastic bottles so that she wouldn't slip in the ice shining crystal clear. She

85

went near the spring, tried to open the tap but couldn't because her hands were freezing. Fati felt pity and got out to help her. He opened the door and shouted: "Lena, give me those plastic bottles, I can fill them with water from the inside as everything is frozen out there. She went close to the door coughing hard. She entered the hall, and from her frozen hands he took the empty bottles, filled them with water and accompanied her up to the front gate. She went towards her house with the wind blowing behind her sending her in the same direction.

Fati got back, lied on the sofa, covered in a blanket staring at the TV, listening to the morning news but thinking about Lena because he knew all her problems. She had two little children;one was two years old and the other a few months. Whereas, Sami, her husband had got fired from his job. He had been working as a worker in a construction company during summer. The poor man would go to the labour market everyday waiting for someone to hire him but this was quite difficult because there were so many people desperated to get a job.

He had found a way to get some money, just to buy bread ans some milk for the children, sometimes even a bottle of oil. Everyday he would go to the Boss. This was the nickname for the person who gave loans of cigarettes to those who sold cigarettes. So Sami was part of this category. He bought cigarettes from the Boss and sold them in the market. The markets were divided in territories and areas. Each seller had his own location, and if he didn't sell any cigarette per day he would bring it back to the Boss and than take it again the following day. Sami's location was the Crossroad Fushë-Kosovë according to the agreement that all the sellers had. Coming back home in the evening with a piece of bread on his arm and free becuase the Serbian officers had not chased him during the day was real happiness for Sami.This, because, all the soldiers were round trying to take away their products and money earned during the day, becuase it was considered an illegal job.

In these conditions, the job Sami was doing was a very good and appropriate one because, at least, there were no problems from him concerning the government.

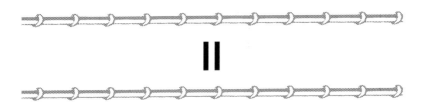

II

As Fati was lying in the sofa, watching TV the phone rang. He answered and the voice of a woman was heard. "It's Zepa, Lena's sister! I'm calling from Germany. I hope you and your family are all well. I would like to speak to Lena if it is possible." Fati remembered this woman, though he had never seen her. She would call often and talk to her sister thorugh Fati's phone. She asked the same, to talk to her sister, but Faik said that there was noone of the children home that he could send to Lena, so he asked her if he could give her a message, but the woman insisted on talking to her sister, though he said that he had just seen her and she was fine. The woman hung up the phone uncontented.

-Hello, Hello!...

Putting down the phone Fati felt bad for the way he answered to the woman, moreover for what he heard on the news that people in an area of Gjilan were in desperate need of help becuase the man of a family was injured and his six little children needed to survive. He felt so sorry and such pity for Lena and her husband that had two very little children. The house they lived in was completely isolated and with no condition. He felt ashamed for not letting the two sisters talk to one another, and felt so terrible with him.

The bad news on TV made him feel worse and worse. He blamed himself:

-Ah, what did I do! Shame on me, shame on me, shame on me! He continued to make self-accusations! Now it was late, regret didn't solve the problem.

As soon as the TV news finished, the phone rang again. The same voice from the other side.

"Please- she said-please can you tell my sister that I have sent her some clothes and medicine and that she should go tomorrow at the bus station"Kosova Raissen" to get them. Fati apologized to her and asked her to call ten minutes later promising her that Lena would be there waiting for her. He apologised again, and the woman was happy to hear that she could now speak with her sister.

From the voice she seemed quite happy and thanked Fati saying:

"Thank you very much, you have always been nice people to us, you and your wife of course! Thank you!

-Well, now I'll go and tell Lena that you called and she will be here right back.

Fati stood up, put on the warm long coat, put on his shoes and went to the small house of Lena and her husband. There was only one room, a very old one room house where the roof was almost ruined.

This house actullay was owned by a relative of Sami who at the time lived in Austria. He went near the gate; only the voice of children crying was heard. He knocked, waited becuase he was sure they didn't hear because of the children crying. Once more he knocked. Now Sami appeared.Pale…. there was a terrible smell inside the house…

There were fumes in the ceiling of this onlyone room house. Apparently something was being burned there, something like clothes. There was this awful smell of plastic and amoniac coming from the stove full of stuff they had gathered from the streets and had been given from people. In the end of the room there was a window made of plastics in blue colour which shadowed the light coming from the window creating half of darkness in it though it was still midday. Fati was baffled in front of such a miserbale scene. It seemed like there was no way to get out of the mysery there. He just couldn't believe what he was watching. This image seemed like an animal stable… Somewhere in the room there was a pile of clothes, old clothes and plastic stuff. In the middle of the room there were pieces of sponge. From the corners of the walls there was humidity.

So, Fati found himself standing at that door, shocked to what he saw. He greeted Sami and told him the reason he was there. Sami went to tell his wife Lena. She got out with the little baby in her arms. They seemed like one single body. He touched smoothly the baby's cheeks, and felt warmth, from the high temperature.

He looked at her and noticed a few wrinkles apparently added to her beautiful face. It seemed like she was getting older and wrinkled ahead of time. Fati, in front of this drama causing real trauma, once more repeated what he said to Sami:

-Nepa, your sister from Germany wants to talk with you on the phone a few minutes later. She will call back.

Putting his hand in the coat pocket he took out the key and said:

-Here is my house key. Go and talk to your sister. I will stay here helping Sami until you come back.

Lena took the keys and the put three months old baby in the middle of the room, next to her older daughter with curly hair, who was sitting down on the ground playing and immediately raised her hands towards her mother who went to talk to her sister Nepa. Lena rushed to the neighbour's house to talk to her sister. After she left the children started sobbing loudly.

Though living next to each other for so many years it was the first time that Fati entered in such a poor house. Children cried asking for their mother. Sami and Fati tried to calm them down but it was almost impossible. The two-year daughter apparently had caught a cold due to the cold weather, humidity smell and fumes of the carbon dioxide coming out from the plastics and old clothes. She cried and coughed scared, constantly asking for her mother back. She looked tired and unhappy, like she was almost giving the goodbye to this life, whereas the little baby of just some months old was lying like a baby doll. Now she had no voice coming out of her tiny body. She was sleeping. On the very old stove Sami had put an old frying pan made of black plastic. It seemed like it was infected. Inside of the pan there was a red pickled pepper and he was trying to cook it. It seemed like pepper was being cooked just to make him feel angry. It seemed like it was in the shape of a fish which jumped around and wanted to get out of the pan. It almost couldn't fit in that place and jumped up high because of the bug bubbles of oil mixed witg wated. It blew off over the old stoe which Sami had lit using some old clothes such as old shoes, plastic dishes taken from the rubbish bins outside in the streets. He always lit the fire using these things, both for cooking and warmth, but they caused such a fume that was an awful mixture of all these products and caused loud cough.

-Oh my God! What is this?! How is it possible to live in such conditions?! We are living in the end of century!

He was so emitional being in front of this image of a cruel reality. He felt so bad being a witness of the sacrifice of two young parents in such economic conditions without any financial source and future perspective. He drew his attention

-What you are burning here is unhealthy, especiallly for your children.

Sami reasoned his actions:

-I know that, but we do not have woods and we don't have money to buy bread for our children. We have had a power cut since six months.

At that moment Lena came, seeming happy from the conversation she had done with her sister in Germany. She told Sami:

-Appareny she has sent us sone clothes and medicine for the children.

She handed in the keys and thanked Fati from the bottom of her heart. The children, as soon as they saw their mother they immediately calmed down and ran to her happily.

Fati coughing, together with the others who were there got out of the home very desperate amd troubled for what he saw in that house ans in that family. Now he challenged himself to help this family get out of misery. He thought: "As main neighbour, I have everything, whereas these people are suffeeing in these conditions, suffering for what is most necessary in life. How can this be possible?! He just couldn't calm down. Desperated he kept asking himself questions: "How come that I had no idea of this? How come that I didn't know what happens in this family?" It's a pity that many people know nothing about how others around them try to make out a living! He imagined the verses of Migjeni *"Bukuria që vret"* written amd lived ninety years ago. He couldn't just sit in his room. He thought: "Why not go and take those people, bring them in my home until the situation improves? As my wife and children are not at home there is enough space for us all. The room is big enough ans there is the stove and woods enough to pass these cold days." He stood up, opened the door and went back to Sami's home. He asked them to go to his home like he was giving them an order. From the loud crying of their children Sami didn't quite understand what he was saying so he asked him to repeat. Fati was patient enough to clarify his idea to him.

-I suggest you should come in my home for three days until my family is back.

In the beginning they refused but he insisted in such way that to some point they were obliged to agree. Fati was persistent in his idea that the whole family should go with him in his house until the weather conditions improved, and then they would think about an appropriatw solution. Each of them took a child in their arms and left.

In this house everything was different. There were no fumes, no carbon dioxide. Fati opened the door and said:

-Feel home! You can rest here in this big room. He put woods in the stove and lit the fire. He asked Sami to take as many woods as he needed. There were sofas all around the room so that the peopld could sit and take a nap there. He also showed them the toilet which they could use whenever needed.

-You are like members of my family until the moment you stay here. Regarding food there is enough here in the fridge so feel free to eat whatever you want as much as you want.

The children looked better, but they still coughed hard. They had taken a cold there in their house. Now, the stove was reddish and warm.

The following day the storm was over. Temperatures were a bit higher, over 0 grades celcius.

Fati couldn't sleep all night. He had nightmares, because of the thoughts of how to find a choice to help this poor family in this emergency. It was Sunday. He decided to help the family as soon as he could with material help because time went by and this family really needed help. He considered this very sincerely. Helping others is a virtue that is innated with humanity and is strengthened along his life. Unfortunately he couldn't fulfill all the duties he thought about, though he considered this action very honestly and sincerely. He started acting however, thinking of some neighbours who were in good economic conditions and whom he thought of as potential helpers. He believed they would be supportive in such situation. Without thinking too much he went to see them. He knocked on all gates asking for support to help Sami and his family. He felt sorry and pity about the case of Sami whom he had seen with his own eyes and had welcomedin his home until the weather improved. Most of the people knew Sami but they had never seen him in such siituation. The fact that Fati brought him at his house was a string argument, because he brought them far from that cold cottage. This convinced those who wanted and had the possibility to help. They could not hesitate in such occasion. The project Fati started within the neighbours was welcomed by almost everyone. They supported this initiative considered positive by all the villagers. Finally the great day was there. Different materials were gathered, more than Fati had thought of.

Two days after Sami thanked Fati for the shelter and help. When temperatures started to improve he asked to go back to his cottage. The snow now was melting and shelters were leaking. Fati insisted that the family stayed at his home, and to feel free and comfortable there.

-You are very welcome here, -he said, -on the contrary I am happy for having you here.

-No, Fati, Sami replies - tomorrow your family will be here and we don't want to stay here and impede you. Moreover now the weather seems much better.

-Ok then, -Fati said to Sami. I agree.

-Before you leave, please take this carriage and load it with woods. Load three carriages and take them with you at home. Don't continue burning that stuff, it is not healthy at all.

Fati helped Sami load the carriages, they sent them to the house of Sami who then got back, took the kids and his wife thanking Fati with all his heart for everything.

Two days later it was a market day in Fushë Kosovë. Fati with the materials he had gathered, with the money he had, went to the market quickly and there he bought five m^3 of woods. He also went to a grocerie, whose owner was Ali. There he took 300 kg floor, rice, pasta, sugar, 20l of oil. After taking the money for the sold products, the shopkeeper Ali asked:

-Why are you buying so much? Are you getting married again? - And he started laughing again.

Fati replied:

-These are for Sami.

-Who is Sami?

-The man who stands here, in front of your shop, every day, and sells cigarettes.

-Really!! - Ali asked surprised.

-Yes, yes, - Fati answered,-we gathered this money together from some donators who are our neighbours. We will help him because he needs food and woods for the winter.

-Really?! -He stepped back. - Sorry, maybe my joke was inappropriate.

-It's ok, - Fati said.

-Well, I want to give my help for Sami too, because I know the poor guy. He comes everyday here in front of the shop to sell cigarettes or to find a job. Just a moment, I'll bring something too.

He hurried and brought a big carton package. Inside it there was some food, three kg of sausages, sixty eggs, five kg chicken meat, two kg of tea and coffee and gave them to Fati.

-These are from me.

Moreover he took out 100 german marks.

-Give him this money too. I know him well.

He spoke proudly hugging him:

-Fati, well done! You have done a great job. We should help each other. Today or never!

Nearby was the office of Electricity Bills Payment. Fati paid the debt that Sami owed to Elektro - Kosovë. It was one year and half that he hadn't paid.

He begged the accountant to send someone who could reconnect the energy. He immediately agreed.

Ali said to Fati:

-I have a proposal.

-Tell me, - Fati replied.

-Wecan leave the floor to Idriz, the baker. I am sure he will accept so Fati can go there and get bread whenever he needs until the floor finishes.

-Good idea. We'll ask Idriz.

Idriz accepted quickly. They gave him 300 kg of floor. He agreed that Sami went there whenever Sami needed bread. -Here he has 300 kg floor. Whenever he needs he can come and get bread from you.

They brought all these products in Sami's cottage with the small vehicle loaded with woods. Before arriving at the cottage the seller told Fati:

-Ehe, I will give him 2 m^3 of woods for free and I'll come back next week to bring them.

Not yet had Fati arrived Sami's house with the electricity bill paid, the electricians came to fix the cables for reconnection. The carriage entered the garden of the house. Sami got out of his home, surprised of what he saw. He couldn't believe his eyes. Fati said:

-These are for you, Sami.

-Let's load the woods and the other stuff.

A very nice and beautiful smile appeared in Fati's pale face. He got a totally different view. When they handed in the food and woods for warmth Sami and Lena couldn't believe their eyes. They were so surprised and couldn't keep to the emotions. Their eyes filled with joy and tears. After putting everything out in the garden Fati neared to the couple Sami and Lena. He handed the money which were left: 720 german frangs and 490 swiss frangs.

-This money is for you in case you need them in the following days.

He also asked Sami to go to the bakery of Idriz any time he needed bread.

-You can get your everyday bread there as you have been deposited 300 kg floor until all this is consumed and he keeps evidence of this.

Sami in sign of gratitude bent in front of Fati. Kneeling down he directed his hands towards the sky and prayed to God with these words:

"Dearest God! Please help and save this good man whenever he is in difficulty!"

Fati answered:

-This is our moral obligation and it wasn't only me who did this, but other neighbours helped too. I just took the initiative but they gave great support, because initiatives without support can not be realized. These people are Nevzad, Hazir, Imam Nuhiu, Enver, Ismet, Fadil, Bejta, Ali, Idriz the baker. This gentleman standing here will also bring two more meters of woods free of charge the next week. Before they left, he got back once more, put his hand in the pocket and took out the electricity bill he had paid for the annual debt. From the other pocket he took out the list with the names of all people who helped in this humanitarian activity. He got out of the yard happy and proud for everything he had done in the name of human mission supported by his very generous and good-hearted neighbours.

MUSTAFË ISMAILI

Toronto, July 2017

95

Printed in the United States
By Bookmasters